FROM GAZA, WITH LOVE

A Novel

Based on a True Story

ZAMAN MADHI

From Gaza, With Love
Copyright © 2024 Zaman Madhi

All rights reserved.

First Edition.

ISBN: 979-8-218-41178-7

Front Cover: 123rf.com/videoflow; /olandsfokus; /studio3321

EMERGING
INK SOLUTIONS
www.emergingink.com

To all the peace-lovers and peacemakers of the world,
And to the Palestinian and Israeli children,
May your future be peaceful.

CHAPTER 1

SAMMY STOOD LOOKING OUT THE window of the kitchen, admiring his work in the backyard. The grass was cut to perfection. Though the yard was not large, it was well-designed with flowerbeds situated at such an angle that Sammy could see their flowers from the kitchen window. It was early June, and new life was everywhere. The trees were full of fresh green leaves. Countless birds filled the sky, flitting among boughs and filling the air with their songs.

With a sigh, Sammy glanced at the framed picture across the room. The photo had been taken by his roommate, Michael, and showcased the beach in the Gaza Strip where a large collection of sea gulls flew over whitecapped waters. The picture captured the exact part of the beach where Sammy had once played and daydreamed. He had always admired the framed beauty as it reminded him of his family and friends and the years of his youth that he had spent growing up in Gaza.

As Michael took a phone call from his mother in his room, Sammy finished washing the dishes, peering out the window to scrutinize his recent yard work. Michael's herb garden was flourishing, which bode well for them, as Sammy and Michael both enjoyed using herbs in their cooking. The roses in the flower garden appeared healthy with innumerous buds. Though nothing was blooming just yet, the sight was promising.

Tea after dinner was a tradition. Sammy placed a teapot to warm on the stove and then wandered outside to the mint patch. After touching and smelling the tender leaves, Sammy picked a couple of the freshest sprigs and then headed back to the kitchen.

His eyes briefly caught sight of the tear-away, daily calendar hanging near the refrigerator. Mint leaves still in hand, he crossed the kitchen and removed the previous day's page so the new date of the 1992 calendar could be read. He sighed. "Already June sixth… Where did the time go?"

Pushing aside the sudden onslaught of emotions that rushed to him, Sammy returned to the kettle to brew the mint sprigs. He liked his tea in a very specific way—black with fresh mint served in a transparent glass to permit him to see the pleasing color of the beverage. He always added two heaping spoonfuls of sugar.

While growing up in Gaza, his younger sister, Miriam, used to make tea and serve it to the family next to the lemon tree in the courtyard of their home. It had always been delicious. Sammy tried to imitate it, but his creations just weren't the same. Her secret might have been her peaceful and joyful spirit.

Once brewed and properly served, Sammy carried his tea to the back patio to admire the sunset. It was almost dusk, his favorite time of the day. The sky was turquoise and was dotted with a few white and orange clouds. Sipping his tea, he tracked songbirds as they retired to neighboring tree limbs and nests for the evening, always chirping and singing. Perfect harmony.

Though he did not live alone, he often felt isolated. He didn't have close friends, and Michael, his roommate, was a friend, but because of their significant age difference, Sammy found it difficult to treat him as a peer. Of course, Chicago was a lively place and Sammy often enjoyed the nightlife that the city offered, but he remained perpetually conflicted about it.

Not only was he concerned about being seen by coworkers, but he was worried that he might give in and engage physically with another man. It was a well-known fact that HIV was wreaking havoc on the national gay community. Thousands were already dead. He had seen it firsthand. Michael's partner, Joseph, had died of AIDS two years prior.

Though tempted to enjoy his time clubbing and dancing, Sammy was terrified. Occasionally, he gave in to his temptations and would go out to enjoy the dancing, music, and community, but he never engaged with anyone sexually. More often than not, most weekends he chose to rent a movie and stay home. And when nobody was looking, he would sneak into the pornographic section of the video store and rent a dirty film.

Tonight, though, he felt the urge to go out.

Gently swirling his tea, he considered where he should go. He favored Roscoe's, a club in Boystown, and decided that's where he would go. He finished his tea shortly before nine o'clock, cleaned the cup, and headed for his bedroom.

Their rental home in the Chicago suburb was small but neat. While Michael primarily took care of the shopping and cooking, Sammy cleaned and tended to the yard. It was a comfortable team effort.

Sammy's room was modestly furnished with a bedroom set that had been gifted to him by Michael and Joseph ten years prior when he had first arrived in America. The top of the dresser was cluttered with colognes and moisturizers as well as a book and a small, framed black-and-white faded Polaroid photo. The picture was of an old man and woman who wore the signs of time and age on their faces.

Sammy breathed deeply as a pleasant breeze wafted through the open window across the room. He smiled at the picture, reverently picked it up, gave it a small kiss, and then returned it to its perch. Determined to get in the mood, he turned on Michael Jackson's "Madonna" and started singing and dancing in rhythm before his mirror.

He was satisfied with what he saw. His face was clear and sported a permanent tan with high, rosy cheekbones. When he smiled, his dimples made him look sexy and attractive. His brownish-red hair was always cut short and perfectly combed.

"I haven't been out in the sun yet this year," he said to himself. "My tan isn't that deep. I guess people will think I'm white… That'll make it easier for me to blend in. But what am I going to do with my accent?" He continued to study himself in the mirror.

Some people liked his accent, but it always raised questions. Sammy didn't like to talk about it and hated to lie. He considered just dancing and not talking.

"Just have a few drinks, dance, and come back home," he told himself.

After a quick shower, he dressed, checked himself in the mirror a few more times, and then hurried out to his car before he could change his mind.

He spent the drive downtown glancing at himself in the mirror. When he reached Halsted Street, he found the road packed with cars and pedestrians. Music and chatter filtered from the numerous clubs and bars that lined the street. Clothed in the latest fashions or flamboyantly dressed, men meandered along the sidewalks, laughing and talking loudly.

Unable to find a parking spot, Sammy ventured a few blocks over where he found the pedestrians there dressed predominantly in leather. Around the corner, he chuckled upon spotting other men sporting country western outfits with ten-gallon hats and cowboy boots. He parked and watched, intrigued by the alternative lifestyles of the gay community.

After checking his face one last time in the pull-down mirror, Sammy got out and headed for Rosoce's near eleven o'clock, the time when most clubs started to get busy. There was a short line there. His ID was quickly checked before he was ushered in without issue.

He looked around—there were the same faces, the same people. Avoiding eye contact, he strode straight to the dance floor, which was packed like usual. Moving with the music, he worked his way through the throngs of people until he was in the center of the crowd. He allowed the music and lights to consume him.

He was so into his dancing that he barely noticed that a young man with sensitive blue eyes had begun dancing in front of him as if they were together. As their gazes met again and again, they drew closer, the space between them disappearing as they danced to each song.

The man was lean and of the same height as Sammy and moved with deliberate ease. Though the club was dark, Sammy glimpsed the nice jeans and designer shoes between them when he wasn't staring into the stranger's eyes. The young man's brown hair was cut short and neat. While everyone else smelled of cigarettes and alcohol, this stranger bore the scent of lavender and clean skin.

A certain tension arose between them, each waiting to see if the other would speak. Sammy finally broke the silence by suggesting a break. They moved to the bar and ordered drinks.

"My name is John," said the no-longer stranger, extending his hand.

"I'm Sammy."

They talked for a while about the bar, the people, the music, and the weather, agreeing that it was a perfect summer night. The bar was getting stuffy and smoky, so John suggested they take a walk to get fresh air. They made their way outside and strolled toward the park by the lakefront.

It was deserted as already midnight had passed. No one was supposed to be there at that time, but Sammy and John kept walking.

Nervous, Sammy suggested, "Maybe we should go somewhere else? Maybe a different club?"

John chuckled and pointed out another couple walking through the park. "The police won't bother us; they just look the other way. Besides, we're only walking."

They continued in tense silence before Sammy eagerly pointed out a large tree. Laughing, he ran to it and climbed up to sit on one of the thick, low-hanging boughs.

"What are you doing? You must be crazy," joked John. "Come on down. You could fall."

"No… I like it. I used to climb a lot of trees as a kid. Can you climb up here?"

"I'll try," said John. Sammy extended his hand and helped his new friend up the tree. John situated himself next to Sammy, and they observed the quiet park. It was dark, pleasant.

Sammy glanced at John. "You are beautiful. I'm glad you danced with me."

"I'm glad I danced with you too. I wanted to touch you, but I felt I should wait."

Sammy said, "You can touch me now."

John's gentle touch became a sheepish kiss. Feeling a connection with this new friend, Sammy deepened the kiss. An hour passed, and they didn't know it. They were so enthused by the other that they almost fell from the tree. Laughing, they caught themselves and climbed down.

Realizing the evening was over, Sammy began feeling anxious once more as they began to leave the park. He couldn't help his quickened pace or jittery movements.

Placing a gentle hand on Sammy's shoulder, John stopped him. "I live close. Why don't you come over? You can drive home tomorrow morning."

Surprised and appalled, Sammy coldly pulled away. "I've never slept over at a stranger's house. I don't do that."

Obviously disappointed, John said, "Well, maybe we can meet for dinner sometime?"

Sammy regarded him warily in the light of the streetlight. This was exactly what he had feared might happen if he went to Boystown. Temptation had come calling. The picture on his dresser flashed in his mind.

His experience at the park had been fine, like a pleasant fantasy. But for Sammy, the idea of having a relationship was not something he believed in. His idea of having an affair with a man stopped right there at the edge of the park.

Ignoring John's invitation, he rushed on, walking fast to his car. He was afraid to give in to his desires. He looked back at John and said, "I will see you again one of these Saturdays at the club. It was fun being with you."

Sammy saw John give a short wave and then, shoulders weighed with disappointment, turn to walk away.

The car ride home was a miserable affair as Sammy drowned in his thoughts. He had enjoyed John's company but couldn't imagine having a relationship with a man who would last more than one brief encounter.

Having sex with a man is impossible, he thought to himself. *It's like playing Russian roulette. I will just keep it the way it is.*

Once home, he went straight to his room and stood before the photo. "Why did you let me go to America?" he asked the people frozen in time within its frame. "I could have stayed home and become a fisherman like everybody else in the village. I would have been married with children." He sighed. "Life in America is so… difficult. I'm trying, but I cannot find myself. I need guidance. I need your advice."

Not for the first time, he closed his eyes and tried to imagine himself married with a wife and children.

After a moment, he frowned. "No, that's not me. It could never work." Disgusted with himself and the situation, he moved to turn off the light. "Whatever will be will be."

He spent the night restlessly tossing and turning in bed. His brain remained preoccupied with the thoughts of living his life based on a new reality, new culture, new location, new people. It made him feel liberated dreaming of doing the things that he enjoyed, the things that were banned or not tolerated within the confines of Palestinian society. The restrictions and rules of his culture were like heavy chains that controlled his every move.

Being gay was completely against his upbringing. He could never have lived his life the way he wanted to had he stayed in Gaza. In his village, everyone had known everything about everyone, and no one had talked about sex, especially homosexuality.

Though in Chicago he was permitted to explore and learn about such taboos, he remained shackled by the rigorous cultural codes he had been brought up under. "It's wrong, it's wrong," he whispered to himself. "I can't do it."

In the morning, Michael called from downstairs, "Coffee is ready! It looks like a nice day today! Let's sit on the patio."

Sammy slowly made his way down the staircase to sit outside. He shared with Michael what had happened the previous night. Since he had met his roommate years ago while growing up in Gaza and had faced the cultural acclimation of America with him, Sammy felt relaxed enough to be vulnerable with Michael.

"My advice," Michael said, "is to create a balance between the two cultures. It's terrible to hate yourself for the things that come naturally to you. If you see John again, go out with him and see where it goes."

Distressed by his answer, Sammy shook his head and settled his gaze elsewhere within the yard. "I don't know if I can do that." The conversation ended there.

After finishing his coffee, Sammy went up to his room and closed the door behind him. Struggling to keep the expression on his face even, despite the pain in his heart, he went again to the photo on the dresser and swept it into a tight hug. "What should I do?" he whispered.

He exchanged the photo for a book, a copy of the Quran, which he also held tightly to his chest.

"Nothing I do is right. I know you disapprove of my behavior. It goes against everything I learned when I was a child and what my religion told me. I need to change."

Unable to keep the tears at bay, he lay down in bed and cried. The thought of going to a psychiatrist to become a straight man crossed his mind a few times, although he had heard that therapies of conversion never worked. Despite that, he still considered it.

Sammy spent the week focused on work; occasionally, John's face flashed in his mind, but he stubbornly pushed it away. For a few weeks, he managed to stay away from the clubs, avoiding the possibility of running into John. Instead, he sat in his room Saturday nights, playing his favorite music and keeping himself occupied with memories of his childhood years, his parents, and his siblings whom he had not seen since he left Gaza.

He had learned to be satisfied with infrequent phone conversations with his parents as their home in Gaza did not have a phone. His parents had to visit the post office in Gaza City and arrange for a pricey, three-minute-long international call.

Of course, he sent what money he could to them. The life of a fisherman was difficult. Sometimes there was nothing to sell, only to eat. The only aid that came through was from the United Nations Relief Fund for Palestinian Refugees in the form of basic food supplies. Without that, they went hungry. Refugees got a monthly ration of flour, rice, beans, and cooking oil—hardly enough to cover the whole month. His parents had to allocate portions to make the supplies last. Some days, they went with less food. Growing up, Sammy himself had gone to bed hungry. There was not enough for everyone.

In every rushed phone conversation, his mother reminded him to eventually return home so he could marry a local village girl. "You come marry a girl from your own heritage, your own religion," she would say. "Don't marry an American girl."

On his lunch breaks, Sammy made it a point to take walks and window shop along the Magnificent Mile. One day a few weeks later as he meandered along the main thoroughfare admiring the store displays, he was startled from his thoughts by a hand on his shoulder. He whirled around to find John. His heart skipped a beat before he blushed.

With a grin, John warmly greeted him.

Though thrilled to see John, Sammy chided himself to remain cool and aloof.

"I haven't seen you in the clubs recently," said John. "You must have found the man of your life. You just disappeared from the scene."

"Man… of my life?" asked Sammy. "That's not going to happen. I'm happy by myself."

"Oh, my mistake." John shuffled awkwardly. "So… you're not coming back to the clubs? You told me you enjoyed music and dancing. Right?"

Sammy struggled to keep his tone even. "Maybe one day. I have to be in the right mindset. I'm still recovering from our first encounter."

John frowned. "What do you mean?"

"I feel like being with a man is like playing with fire. I love the warmth and the closeness and the comfort, but I know logically it's going to burn me."

John continued to regard him for a moment and then sighed. "I'll be at the club next Saturday around eleven. On the dance floor. Think about it, Sammy. I don't need an answer right now."

Sammy fidgeted as he felt his composure fracture. Holding John's gaze, he finally said, "I'll be there."

Sammy returned to his office deep in thought. *There's something about John that I like. I feel comfortable looking into his eyes. I feel safe being close to him. There's something about him… I'll meet him and see where it goes, just like Michael said. I'll be open, frank, and totally honest. Hopefully… he'll do the same.*

The rest of the week passed slowly.

When Saturday finally arrived, Sammy was a nervous mess. After checking himself in the mirror, yet again, he applied a touch of gel and then a spritz of cologne. He glanced at the treasured picture of his parents. "I know you don't approve of this, but there's nothing I can do about it now. I'm not changing; I'm the same Sammy you know. I love you."

He rushed downstairs and drove to Halsted Street.

The sidewalks were packed like before. Lines of people filed through standing doors, waiting to get into the clubs. Sammy was lined up outside Roscoe's when John joined him. "We're going to have a great evening," John beamed. "You look good, Sammy."

Half the people in the long line were smokers. Sammy pulled out a package of cigarettes and offered one to John, who reluctantly took it. "I smoke occasionally and only this brand."

"I only smoke when I come out to the clubs," explained Sammy. "A cigarette goes well with a drink."

The line was long, far longer than he had expected, which gave Sammy time to start fretting. As he puffed on his cigarette in discomfort, he reflected on his nervousness.

"We could go somewhere else," suggested John, seeming to notice his fidgeting.

"This is my favorite club. I really don't like the others," Sammy argued. "Besides, they have lines."

John laughed. "Then how about the tree?"

Sammy thought about it and then, with a smile, nodded.

As they walked to the park together, John extended a hand. Hesitantly, Sammy accepted it. The streets were crowded with Boystown enthusiasts. Because this district was a relatively safe one, gay men could comfortably walk the streets without the threat of harassment.

Sammy glanced at John. He took in his confidence, his deliberate steps, how well he was put together. A small piece of Sammy admired him. His enormous, blue eyes were enchanting.

"They must be gay homes," John remarked, pointing out houses' beautifully kept gardens along the way. "Look how manicured they are. It's not a stereotype; it's true!"

Using the underground path, they crossed Lakeshore Drive.

"It's so humid," Sammy murmured. "I hope it doesn't rain. There's only a thirty percent chance of rain according to the weatherman."

John chuckled. "No, no rain tonight. It's just hot and humid, and we're going to have a lot of fun."

Pointing to the tree, they laughed loudly and ran toward it. Once they had scrambled up to the same branch where they had sat before, they continued to hold hands. To the east was Lake Michigan, a dark and quiet place. To the west was Lakeshore Drive, bustling with noisy cars and sirens. Although it was almost midnight, it was loud.

Sammy swallowed, anxiety once again rearing its ugly head. The noise was almost too much.

Suddenly, a motorcycle revved down Lakeshore Drive with an earsplitting roar, disturbing everything in the vicinity, including the birds nesting in the tree.

A cold sweat broke over Sammy as he started to tremble. The din reminded him of the military vehicles that frequented the main road near his family's house. The armored vehicles, which often reverberated down the streets, always scared him as they meant something was wrong. Usually, their passage was followed by a volley of gunshots.

Loud noises, even thunderstorms, made Sammy nervous. If he was driving, he would pull over and wait until the thunder had passed.

"Sammy?" John leaned into him. "What's wrong? Your hands are cold. You're shaking. What's wrong?"

"No, nothing," Sammy murmured.

Struggling to calm himself, Sammy wiped his face. John wrapped an arm around him, rubbing his shoulder comfortingly. After several long moments of silence, he slowly pressed his cheek against Sammy's and then kissed him. Sammy's fears subsided.

"Hm?" Sammy drew away suddenly. "Do you feel that?"

"What?"

"A drop of water."

John peered upward. "There's only a slight chance of rain tonight. We should be able to stay here for a while—"

A sudden bolt of lightning split the air; a low grumble of thunder pealed after it. Both flinched in the tree. A gust of wind shifted the heavy branches as a sheet of rain poured from the sky.

Together, they jumped from the tree and started to run for the underground crossing. By the time they were safely there, they were soaked.

"Even my underwear is wet!" laughed John, pushing his wet hair from his forehead. "You look like you just got out of the shower. Let's go to my place. At least you can dry your clothes."

Sammy forced himself to say, "Yes."

As the rain pitter-pattered around them, they strode hand-in-hand to John's apartment in the heart of Boystown. The building was luxurious and boasted perfect everything—flowers, entrance, carpet, lighting. Everything was clean and shiny.

John led him to a door on the second floor. Sammy hesitated mid-step as he spotted a mezuzah hanging on the doorframe. *Of all people, he's Jewish*, Sammy thought in disbelief.

The apartment was spacious and well-furnished. A piano with a menorah atop it acted as the centerpiece of the abode. There was no question in Sammy's mind that this was a Jewish home.

Growing uncomfortable, he weighed his options. *Should I tell John I'm Palestinian?*

The Jewish people he had once met with Michael and Joseph had been very kind and welcoming. They had been part of an organization called Peace Now, which strived to create peace and harmony between Israel and Palestine. Sammy had found their beliefs to be similar to his own and had relished visiting with them. But this was different. Perhaps his new acquaintance would not be so hospitable.

John offered Sammy a robe so he could put his clothes in the dryer.

"I'll stay here until my clothes are dry," Sammy announced, "and I will be sitting in the living room."

Amused, John nodded and replied in his usual calm manner, "If that's what you want. We can just talk."

As Sammy meandered around the apartment, taking in the photos on the walls and the flowers perched on the counter in the kitchen, he considered his predicament.

"Before you sit, why don't I show you around?" John offered. And he did just that. They walked around the apartment, and he described everything around them, every piece of furniture and every meaningful picture. Eventually, John pointed at a picture of a young man in a small frame. "This is a picture of someone I loved. He died of AIDS two years ago."

"Oh, I'm very sorry to hear that," Sammy solemnly replied. But John's explanation made Sammy concerned. Was John HIV positive? If that were the case, he should stop seeing him now. At least he wouldn't have sex with him. Even kissing him became a concern in Sammy's mind.

As if reading his mind, John added, "I'm HIV-negative. I test regularly and am very protective of myself and whoever I'm with."

They sat next to each other on the couch and Sammy said, "I am HIV-negative as well, but I have something very important that I want to share with you. I do not know how you will feel about it. I've noticed that I'm in a Jewish home."

"Yes, I'm Jewish."

Sammy met his gaze. "I'm Palestinian."

There was a long moment of silence before John asked, "So, how do you feel being with a Jewish man?"

Sammy's response was quiet. "Maybe we should stop here."

John stood and began pacing the apartment in thought. "You're the… first Palestinian I've ever met. I only know Palestinians through TV, and it's not flattering." He looked at Sammy. "You don't appear Palestinian, nor do you act like one."

Sammy stood. "Look at me, John. I look Palestinian; I act Palestinian; I eat Palestinian. I'm Palestinian through and through. It's where I was born and raised. It's my parents and grandparents. It's my culture and my heritage." John just gazed at him. With a sigh, Sammy said, "Maybe I should leave. I'm sure the clothes are dry enough."

John crossed the room and embraced him, kissing him deeply. Sammy did not resist, couldn't resist. He held John just as tightly and kissed him eagerly. As he pulled away, he said somberly, "I assume… this is goodbye."

John kissed him again. "No, Sammy. This isn't goodbye. I would like to know more about you." He touched Sammy's face. "I want to get to know you. I'm so… interested in you. I want to know about your life."

Sammy smiled, his heart nearly bursting. He was nervous, but he felt comfort in John's arms and words. "I'll see you again on one condition—no talk of religion or politics."

CHAPTER 2

THE FOLLOWING WEEK, JOHN TALKED with Sammy once a day via phone, usually in the evenings. He was curious about Sammy and wanted to get to know him better. Countless questions crowded his mind alongside the doubt that he could manage such a different relationship. John had legitimate concerns. He was Jewish while Sammy was Muslim and Palestinian. How could any type of trust form between them when they had both grown up hearing about how awful the other was, learning about the atrocities one nation had committed against another, experiencing conflict that often felt personal?

At the end of the week, John convinced Sammy to meet him for dinner on Sunday evening when the restaurants were less crowded. Sammy left the choice of the eatery to John but suggested seafood. Deciding for now that it would be best if they stayed in a safe area, John set reservations at a Boystown seafood restaurant, which was owned by a gay couple and frequented by gay men. It was a place to see and be seen.

Though John was nervous, he wasn't as uncomfortable as Sammy apparently was. He found his date's jitteriness endearing.

The waiter pointed them to a table by the window, which Sammy politely declined. They ended up seated close enough to the window to see the street but far enough away so as not to be seen from outside. John gave Sammy a quick embrace before sitting and peering into his hazel eyes.

Sammy was tense. He shifted in his chair and glanced anxiously over his shoulder. With a chuckle, John took his fingers and warmly rubbed the top of Sammy's hand. He was pleased when Sammy seemed to relax after that.

"Now we can talk," Sammy said, glancing at the menu. "I'm sure you want to know more about me, just like I want to know more about you."

"That's true," replied John. "Let's order first and then chat."

It took but a few minutes for them to decide on appetizers and main courses and submit their order to a nearby waiter.

"Okay," said John as the waiter walked away. "Start from wherever. I'm here to listen."

Sammy grinned uncomfortably. "I'll try to make it short, but it is a long story." He gave a nervous laugh. "Maybe we should order wine. That'll loosen me up…" His handsome face grew solemn. "Every time I think about or talk about my childhood, I become sad, tense. I don't know…"

John flagged the waiter and quickly ordered a bottle of wine. "Share with me what you feel comfortable sharing, Sammy," he said, returning his attention to his date. When Sammy didn't say anything, he added, "I want to know about your life, your family, your childhood."

At that, Sammy looked out the window at the sidewalk. After a moment, he pointed at a homeless man shuffling along. "At one point, my parents were homeless."

John fell still.

"My parents were refugees. They fled their hometown of Jaffa when war broke out in 1948. They had only just married. My father was a fisherman."

"Wait," interrupted John. "Jaffa, Israel?"

"No, Jaffa, Palestine. They weren't given time to pack, not that they had much. Their fishing boats were the only things that were of use to them. So, they fled in their boats and ended up at the Gaza shores. And that's where I was born and raised." Sammy shifted in his seat. "My parents and grandparents came from Jaffa. It was the same for everyone else I knew. So, when everyone fled, we all ended up in Gaza on a small cliff that overlooked the Mediterranean."

The waiter returned with the wine and politely served it to them. Once he left, Sammy continued in a more morose tone. His voice shook.

"For the first few weeks, they were literally homeless and lived in the open under a few scattered trees until they were provided tents by the UNRWA. Eventually, the locals helped them build a small shack-like structure with no running water, electricity, or sewage." Sammy nodded. "So, that's where my family is from. And… I'll stop there…" He smiled at John. "I want to know about you now."

Still processing it all, John began slowly. "I'm very much an American, born and raised here. My life isn't that complicated. My parents are divorced, but I've managed to maintain a good relationship with both of them. I mean, there's nothing difficult about my life, Sammy."

"No, keep going. I want to know more," Sammy encouraged.

Voice low, John said, "Uh, my grandparents—my father's parents—were immigrants from Germany. They fled the Nazis and arrived in the U.S. in the late thirties. My mother's side is Catholic; they're immigrants from Ireland." He chuckled, realizing that he needed to carefully change the subject. "But there'll be more time to talk about our families later, right? Did you see the dish the waiter brought to that table? You're into seafood, right?"

Sammy glanced over his shoulder and smiled. "One of the clearest memories I have is of my mother cleaning fish all the time, especially during sardine season. Every morning, my father would fish for sardines and bring in a haul of them on top of a large wooden tray. My mother would clean each fish in the court of the house where everything was done. She cooked the sardines in different ways but mostly she fried them. Sometimes one of my older brothers would take them to the local bakery to be baked. Oh, I miss eating fresh sardines. I wish they had them here, but I'm sure they don't."

"Sardines *are* big in Chicago," John teased. He was pleased when Sammy chuckled. "You mentioned your brother. How many siblings did you have?"

"I was born into a very crowded household. We are nine all together—four brothers and five sisters. I was number eight. And we had my parents and my grandmother with us." He smiled sadly. "She passed a few years ago… I was number eight, the baby boy of the family, so I was nothing new; my parents had a long line of children before me. I only have one younger sibling, a sister, who is two years my junior. I was born at home, as were all my brothers and sisters, by the same midwife."

"It must have been quite cramped," John replied.

"It was. Most of the rooms were small and had corrugated tin roofs. In the summer, it was too hot; in the winter, it was too cold. When it rained at night, the noise was so loud that I could hardly sleep. The boys slept in one room and the girls in another."

As John ate, he remarked, "Well, that's good." He liked hearing about Sammy's upbringing. Though his own was vastly different, he felt a kinship with the hazel-eyed man.

"Your parents are divorced?" asked Sammy suddenly.

John grimaced, wishing he hadn't said anything. "Yeah, they divorced when I was nine. I was raised by my father's parents." He picked at his food, uncomfortable. "They lived in Nazi Germany and I… got their first-hand accounts of everything. The abuse, the hatred, the Holocaust. They were still reeling from it all and I had front-row seats to it growing up." He shrugged to lessen the pain. "They thought everything would change in America, but living as a Jewish man in the United States can be just as uncomfortable at times."

"Really?" asked Sammy sincerely.

John nodded. "I often hear people talk about Jews, not knowing that I am one. It's not flattering or comfortable. There's so much anti-Semitism in this country… and I don't know why."

A momentary lull visited their table as they continued to eat, each in thought. Eventually, Sammy said with a big smile, "We have a lot in common. You're Jewish. I'm Muslim. We're both circumcised."

John burst into laughter and corrected, "We've yet to find out."

"I am!" Sammy assured him. "I remember clearly the day I was circumcised. I was eight years old. It was a day to celebrate. I was so pampered that day. I was the focus of attention. All my brothers and sisters, uncles and aunts, neighbors—everyone got together in the small courtyard of our house and told me that I was about to become a man and that I couldn't cry. They made a big deal about it. They hired the barber of the neighborhood to perform it. The women celebrated the circumcision with traditional songs." He leaned on an elbow in thought. "They sang about a young boy growing up, becoming a man." He told John, "According to Islam, boys are required to be circumcised. You know, John, I did not cry. I wanted to scream, but I was too proud. It hurt badly though. Every day after the circumcision, I went with my mother to the beach and she would dip me in the salt water. It burned in the beginning, but it helped the healing. Do you remember your circumcision, John?"

John beamed. "I sure do. In some Jewish traditions, especially the orthodox ones, the person is not Jewish unless the mother is. Therefore, I had to go through a conversion. The process of conversion requires circumcision. Actually, I was circumcised as a baby, but I still had to go through the rituals. It was embarrassing. At twelve years old, I had to drop my pants in front of the rabbi. He had to draw blood. It was just a little prick on my schmuck, one drop of blood. I also had to go to a *mikvah*, a ritual for purification to complete my conversion."

John leaned forward and continued.

"It was so embarrassing. I had to stand up naked in front of many people and dip myself into a small pool while everybody watched. I felt that everybody was looking at my private parts." He laughed loudly and asked, "Do you want to see it?"

Sammy's face burned pink as John chuckled.

After dinner, they decided to go for a cocktail.

Strolling down Halsted Street, they peered into store windows which all showcased gay themes. It was a time of frustration and danger as the gay community was in the throes of the AIDS crisis. But signs of optimism in the community were everywhere— encouraging and colorful posters in store windows, single-leaf papers taped to lampposts encouraging safe sex, sign-ups to organize for legislation. Boystown was abuzz with empowering messages.

The streets weren't overly crowded, and there was a sense of unhurried tranquility. Boystown was a diverse place to visit and was well known for its peaceful and accepting atmosphere. In fact, many couples were on the street. Sammy furtively motioned to a white man escorting a lovely black woman into a café.

John nodded to the couple. "Interracial dating and marriage were illegal until the 1960s. Did you know?"

"Here? In America?" asked Sammy. "Well, did you know that marriage between Jews and non-Jews in Israel is not allowed? Usually, couples go to other countries, particularly Cypress, to get married and then come back."

John frowned. "But Israel is a free and democratic state."

Sammy passed him a pointed look. "No talk of politics, remember? I'm just stating facts."

Sensing a change in his mood, John glanced at Sammy who had slowed to a stop.

"Let's skip the drinks tonight," Sammy said. "I don't really feel up to it right now."

"Is it because I spoke of Israel?" asked John.

Sammy gave a noncommittal shrug. Unsurprised but still disappointed, John sighed. He couldn't help his viewpoints and how strongly he felt about Israel. It was how he had been raised. To accept criticism of Israel meant that everything his grandparents had undergone had been for naught. Besides, he had family who lived there. He understood the suffering of the Palestinians; he could even perceive the injustice. But his tie to his family and religion was strong.

It took all his emotional and mental effort to extend a hand to Sammy. Sammy took it, and John pulled him into a hug. When he drew away, he met Sammy's gaze. "I'm trying to understand. I hope you are too. Night, Sammy."

As he turned to walk to his car, he heard Sammy call to him.

"I'm trying as well," Sammy said.

With a smile, John asked, "When are we going to meet again?"

"Next weekend maybe?"

"What about Wednesday evening? For some wine?"

Sammy agreed, "Yes, that's a good idea. I'll come directly from work."

"How is seven o'clock at the Piano Bar?"

"That sounds good."

John grinned. "We have a lot to learn about each other. You know that, right?"

"In time, I'll tell you," replied Sammy.

Sammy drove home in deep thought, oscillating between wistful thinking and despair and self-doubt. He didn't know exactly what or how to tell John about his life.

He liked John. John was a nice person. But could Sammy seriously date him, a Jewish man?

Reflecting on the meal, Sammy sighed. John had made him feel different, special. Usually, when Sammy told people where he came from, they shied away, passing furtive looks of suspicion. On more than one occasion he had lied and said that he had come from somewhere other than Gaza. Of course, he had felt horrible denying his heritage and had gone home ashamed, but it was hard to be Palestinian.

Would John's feelings change the more he learned about Sammy? Even Sammy felt odd when he thought of John as Jewish.

"I'm going to see him Wednesday," Sammy said aloud in the car. He scoffed. "I must really like him or something…" He lost himself in thoughts of John's inquisitive blue eyes and gentle laughter.

When he arrived home, he went to his bedroom and made a beeline for the photo on his dresser. Picking it up, he studied the people in it and then shook his head. "I don't know what to do," he muttered.

He slept restlessly that night, torn between continuing a relationship with John and cutting all ties. Staring at the ceiling at two o'clock in the morning, he admitted aloud once more, "I just don't know what to do."

CHAPTER 3

BEFORE HE MET JOHN, SAMMY had felt no interest in dating. Life had been comprised of work and, when he could occasionally muster the courage to visit Boystown, an evening of dancing. But now that John had entered the picture, Sammy felt unbalanced, restless.

To distract himself, he forced his attention onto gardening, shopping, and reading. Michael and Joseph kept a large collection of books on a wide variety of topics, and so Sammy regularly sought solace in titles just after dusting the bookshelves. He relished reading since, prior to arriving in the United States, he had never had a chance to read beyond that which was required by the school. There were no public libraries in Gaza City, and books in the few bookstores were heavily censored. But as much as he hoped reading would occupy his mind, Sammy found that his thoughts always circled back to John.

"What should I do?" he asked Michael. "Should I say anything?"

"There's nothing to say," his roommate replied. "Wait until Wednesday." Michael always offered sage advice. In his late fifties, the man exuded paternal qualities.

"Wednesday night is such a long time from now," Sammy complained impatiently. As if on cue, the house phone rang. Sammy answered it and breathed out in relief—It was John!

"Hey, I just wanted to call and say hello and confirm Wednesday's date," John said.

Sammy went upstairs to complete the call in the privacy of his bedroom. As they briefly chatted, Sammy worked to keep the nervousness in his voice from seeping through. He was anxious and afraid.

Wednesday night, Sammy arrived at the bar as John strode up. They were escorted to a little table in the corner away from the entrance. After getting drinks, they decided to head out to the beer garden since the weather was pleasant. Blooming flowers of pink and white cascaded from hanging planters to create a romantic environment. Scattered red roses in ornate urns brought warmth to the setting. They found a table in the corner of the garden, which gave them privacy, embraced, and then shared a brief kiss.

"It was really difficult finding a parking place nearby," Sammy lamented, trying to start a conversation.

"Yeah, I think I'm illegally parked. I might get a ticket," replied John.

"Oh, you drove?"

"Directly from work. Were you wanting to go elsewhere?"

Sammy shook his head. "No, I can't stay long. This is fine."

John gestured north. "My apartment's a few minutes from here. Do you want to go there?"

Reluctantly, Sammy nodded.

Conversation in the brief car ride to John's apartment was nearly nonexistent. Sammy knew what was on John's mind because it was on his mind too. He wanted to get closer to him, physically. Although they hadn't known each other for long, Sammy was anxious to discover that aspect of their potential relationship. Still, that sliver of guilt that remained sharp under his ribs bothered him.

"Can I get you a drink?" asked John once they arrived. He collected two beers from the fridge, and they sat next to each other. Sammy sipped the can's contents, his heart hammering. He was so sure John could hear it. John fidgeted anxiously before slipping his hand atop Sammy's.

Flushing with excitement and embarrassment, Sammy glanced at John. With a charming smile, John grasped his fingers and then leaned in and kissed him. "Bedroom?" he asked when he pulled away. Sammy didn't remember answering.

At the bedroom door, they shared a long, passionate kiss before starting to clumsily undress one another. In an instant, they were both naked, tumbling onto the comforter.

Sometime shortly before midnight, Sammy rolled out of bed, a deep, satiated feeling within him. He had experienced his first intimate affair—and they were compatible! *Very* compatible.

"You okay?" asked John, sitting up in bed.

"I've never… experienced anything like that before," Sammy murmured in awe.

"That was lovemaking," replied John smugly. "You sure you can't stay the night?"

Sammy sighed. "No, it's late. I have to go." He flashed a grin at John before dressing.

By the time he made it back to his car and was on his way home, Sammy had started to swing precariously between optimistic elation and the sewers of hopeless guilt. He fantasized about a life with John, about building castles in the air and always being wrapped in John's arms. But his shame kept him from soaring up to those castles to reside within their lofty walls.

Sitting at a stop light, he fidgeted. "No, no, I can't do this," he said aloud. "I shouldn't; it's wrong." He ran his hands over the steering wheel. "God, please help me. *Please*. I can't be in a relationship with a man."

The longer he dwelled on it, the deeper he fell. Such a relationship was a sin, was unimaginably unacceptable. He wanted God to help him change his ways. "But how? I am this way, and I didn't create me. I didn't choose," Sammy murmured through tears as he pulled through the green light.

When he arrived home, he concluded that he needed to end it all before his relationship with John developed further. But the thought alone made his heart quiver with pain. He liked John. He liked the way John spoke and how he touched him. He was a kind and loving man, and Sammy so didn't want to hurt him.

Parked outside the house, Sammy weighed his options. "I can tell him that I just don't know how to be in a relationship with someone." He shrugged. "That's it. He's Jewish and I'm Palestinian Muslim. How can the two mix?" He tried to force himself to smile. "We would have constant misunderstandings and conflicts. It's just not wise." He peered out at the house. "I have decided." And with that, he went straight upstairs, washed up, and went to bed to wrestle with his guilt for the rest of the night.

"So," said Michael the following morning over breakfast, "what's new with you? I didn't see you last night."

"I got in after midnight," Sammy replied dully.

"Anything of interest happen last night?"

Sammy swallowed the lump in his throat. "I'm going to end my relationship with John today." He tried to keep his voice even. "As much as I like him and we are compatible physically, we are so different in other ways. He's Jewish, I'm Palestinian Muslim. How can we be in a relationship? Besides, I don't think I believe in men having relationships. I was not raised to believe in that." He gestured to Michael. "You were raised in a different society, a different culture and religion. As much as you and Joseph taught me to accept myself… I'm still finding it difficult."

Michael's face became thoughtful but not judgmental. "Well, think it over and share your thoughts with me. Let's talk about it. Don't rush your decision. Why don't we talk after you get home from work tonight?"

"I'm not going to call him… Or maybe I should. No, I'll wait."

"But it's hard to wait," Michael kindly offered.

Sammy rubbed his face, stressed. "It's constantly on my mind. I think of him all the time. I have to stop." He stood. "I'm going to get ready for work."

Throughout the day, Sammy pondered on his sexual orientation. He had always thought it was a phase, that it would eventually go away. He was, for the most part, a rational person. He realized that he had been the luckiest child in the neighborhood to have been given the opportunity to emigrate to the U.S. and go to college. He was the envy of all his hometown friends who were predominantly fishermen, unemployed, in jail, or dead. He had never expected to be forced to make such an identity-affirming decision. He hated himself, often.

Sammy was an accountant, and just like in accounting, all the numbers had to make sense and fall into place to create a successful outcome. But when it came to John, he just didn't know where to start calculating.

That evening, he sat with Michael and had a pleasant conversation that put Sammy's racing thoughts at ease. Still, whenever he thought of John, he didn't feel rational. In fact, his emotions overwhelmed him and he became an impulsive person willing to do anything to just feel John beside him.

The following morning, Sammy headed for work. It was a gloomy day in Chicago with gray skies and a drizzle in the air. When thunder rumbled overhead, he didn't hesitate. Even as the wind picked up, he remained focused. Instead of being overwhelmed with memories of old, Sammy felt connected to the turbulence and instability of the weather. It reflected how he felt on the inside.

The storm came on suddenly. Sheets of thick rain cascaded across the city as lightning and thunder reverberated along the horizon. Traffic came to a crawl as people tried to escape the wild winds by parking under overpasses. Still, Sammy remained unfazed. He actually liked the rush the adventure gave him.

Eventually, he arrived at the accounting firm where he worked. Eager to occupy his mind, he got to work, delving into the piles of paperwork that had been assigned to him. Midmorning, his phone rang. It was John.

"Good morning," greeted John. "I was just calling to check on you. Did you get to work okay with the weather?"

"Uh, yeah," replied Sammy uncomfortably.

John sighed in relief. "Oh, good. Well, I thought maybe you'd call work off today."

Sammy struggled to keep his voice calm, even. He didn't want to say the wrong thing. "I rarely miss a day of work. Actually, I would like to talk to you a bit longer, but I have things to do." He thought. "How about around lunch or maybe after work?"

"Sure, whichever works for you," John replied.

"It'll just depend on my schedule. I'll call you when I can. Bye." Sammy stared at the phone for a long moment before hesitantly returning his attention to the spreadsheets before him.

Lunch came, but Sammy didn't make the call. He considered waiting until the end of the day, chewing on his cowardice. Eventually though, after a substantial pep talk and with only five minutes left on his lunch break, he picked up the phone and called John.

"Hey, I can't really talk right now," John replied, obviously occupied. "Something's come up for this evening. Could we chat tomorrow sometime? Friday afternoons I usually have more time."

"That's fine," replied Sammy both relieved and disgruntled.

Friday went by torturously slow. When he could contain himself no longer, Sammy finally called John midafternoon. They spoke about many things, but Sammy was unable to bring up ending the relationship. Ultimately, he stopped by a liquor store and then went home where he found Michael already cooking dinner.

Slumped at the table, Sammy watched Michael at the stove. The kitchen smelled good. He could detect familiar spices and guessed that his roommate was making fish. Spotting the pan, he grinned. "I was right," Sammy said. "It's fish." He held aloft the bottle of wine he had purchased. "This'll go well with it." Michael grinned. "I know a little about wine."

His roommate smiled. "I know, you got that from your mother."

Sammy burst into laughter. "My mother never had a sip of alcohol in her life—neither did my father!" He sat back with a sigh. "You know, I never drank before I came to the U.S. I had never even tasted wine, but I like to think that I'm a fast learner."

"Those wine tasting classes helped," Michael replied. He passed him a wink. "Helped you learn how to bluff, make you sound like a wine connoisseur." He retrieved the bottle of wine from the table and opened it. "So, how are you and John doing?"

Sammy grew somber. "Whenever I talk to him and try to end our relationship, my tongue gets twisted and I can't tell him anything. I don't know John very well; it hasn't even been that long since we first met." He thought of John. "He's interesting, kind, sweet. He's cute and I like him, but I can't imagine myself having a relationship with him."

Michael asked, "Why not?"

"You know my background; you know what I believe. How can I? At times I feel so guilty just being myself, just acting the way I want. I feel ashamed. How can I be involved with a man? For me, it is a religious and cultural issue, and it doesn't seem that I can get over it."

Michael sat across from him to regard him. "Don't rush and do not make any hasty decisions that you might regret. Calm down and think it over. Give it some time. He might ask *you* to end the relationship. How would you feel?"

Sammy fell still, his heart aching. "I would not like that… That would be awful."

"Don't you think John would feel awful, too, if you did that to him?"

"Yes, he probably would, and that is why I'm reluctant to do it."

Michael raised his glass. "Cheers, drink up."

They ate dinner in a comfortable silence.

As they cleaned up, Michael periodically reminded Sammy to stay calm, to not be quick to take action. Though Sammy remained inclined to call John immediately, he appreciated Michael's wisdom. As they settled in to watch television, Sammy admitted, "I'll wait and see where it goes."

That night, he was able to sleep a little better.

CHAPTER 4

The 7:00 alarm turned Sammy out of bed on Thursday morning. In his usual purposeful manner, he showered, dressed, and headed for work. Despite the heavy traffic, he arrived at the accounting firm earlier than usual, something he often took pride in, especially when he was the first to reach the office.

Shortly after 9:00, John called. Suddenly jittery, Sammy worked to keep his voice even. "Maybe we could meet up this evening for a drink or a cup of coffee?" he asked.

"Well, why don't we meet at my place? That way I can cook for us," John countered.

"Oh, I didn't expect that," replied Sammy. After a moment of hesitation, he agreed.

That evening, Sammy stopped by a liquor store on the way over to John's apartment and bought his favorite wine, a Napa Valley product that he only purchased for special occasions.

Sammy hadn't even made it through the apartment door before John embraced him and then planted a not-so-chaste kiss on his lips. Exhilarated, Sammy drew away from him, his eyes gleaming with delight, and passed him the bottle of wine. "I picked this red out. It's from Napa Valley, California." As he went on to describe the vineyard and how beautiful the region was, Sammy nervously paced the kitchen. All thoughts of ending their relationship were gone.

"You're kind of standoffish tonight," said John, glancing over his shoulder at him. "Have a bad day at work?"

"No, not really. It's the end of the week, and I'm a little tired. Just need to unwind."

As John began cooking, Sammy sat at the kitchen table and watched, admiring the ease with which John moved about. "It is unlikely," Sammy eventually said, "that you're cooking pork."

"You're absolutely right. I've never cooked pork. In Jewish tradition, we do not eat pork." He grinned. "But sometimes, I cheat and eat bacon."

"It's the same in the Muslim tradition. We're not supposed to eat pork. But you see me drinking alcohol, which also goes against Islamic traditions." Only the sound of something sizzling filled the silence between them for a long moment. "So, tell me more about yourself. Where is your family? Where were you born? Do you have any brothers or sisters?"

"My turn, huh?" asked John, amused. "Let's see. My parents divorced a long time ago, but you know that. I see my father more often than I see my mother because he lives here in the Chicago area. My father is Jewish, my mother Catholic. That's a combination." He laughed. "They were married for nearly ten years. But their relationship became combative; they quarreled a lot. So, they divorced. Honestly, I was relieved because there was no more fighting in the house, no more daily arguments. I miss being home where both my parents used to be, but that's okay. I spend Christian holidays with my mother and Jewish holidays with my father."

As he stirred the pan's contents, he continued.

"I have one sister who is two years younger than me—Jackie. I haven't seen her in a couple of years though because she lives in California. Once in a while, we'll talk on the phone. We weren't very close. She is married and has two children. She and her husband are both computer engineers. They married after they graduated and moved. Actually, they're both atheists."

"Oh," was all Sammy could think to say.

"My dad's always busy. If he's not focused on his job, he's busy with his girlfriend. He says they're not going to marry, but she lives with him and they've been together for a few years. So, something is working. She treats him well."

"And your mother?"

"Oh, she dates around but isn't seeing anyone steady. I think that's by choice. Her social life is interesting. Most of her friends are academics; well, she's an academic herself, so that makes sense. She teaches at a university." John regarded him from the stove with an impish smile. "Your turn…"

Sammy sighed. "I don't know where to start or what to tell you. My parents aren't academics or lawyers; my father is a fisherman and my mother a homemaker. Neither of them learned to read or write. I have a hard time communicating with them because every time I send a letter, my sister must read it to them. But, uh, they have been married for a long time. It's been so long, in fact, that neither can remember how long." Sammy thought of his family. "At times, I believe they are in love with each other. After raising nine children though, you can imagine how tired they are—and it shows."

"I bet it does," replied John.

Desperate not to get bogged down in memories or else allow the guilt he had been repressing to roam, Sammy looked to change the subject. "The food smells good. What is it?"

"On the way home from work, I stopped at a kosher butcher shop and picked out two pieces of their best filet mignon."

"Oh, the wine will go perfectly then," Sammy beamed.

John studied him for a moment before returning his attention to the stove. "I, uh, wanted to let you know that, uh, you're special to me. I'd like to get to know you better. The more you tell me, the more I understand you."

"I feel the same." Sammy leaned on the table. "Then, let's take turns. You tell me something about yourself and then I'll tell you something about me."

"Deal."

Throughout dinner, they talked and Sammy marveled at John's culinary skills. They kept the conversation light, never venturing into personal details until they were certain that was where the other wanted to go. Only when John poured two more glasses of wine and they headed for the living room did Sammy get the sense that their conversation was about to become more serious.

"We must fulfill the deal," John announced, sitting carefully on the couch so as not to spill his glass. "A story for a story. I'll start, and then you go."

"Okay."

"So, I have one sister. Like I said, we were never close. Neither of us tried to keep in touch or communicate. Maybe I shouldn't talk about her this way, but I just don't feel close to her. With our parents divorced and us kids separated, sometimes it's lonely. But I do have friends, so that's where I'll start. I want to tell you about a close friend I met in college. His name was Adam. No, we weren't lovers, just friends. He was such a sweet person. Cute and intelligent. He was successful in school and was hired immediately after college and started making a lot of money. Above all though, he was kind and caring, and I loved him so dearly.

"Four years ago, Adam called me one night, saying that he needed to see me. It was something very serious, I could tell. I went to him. He looked so defeated, depressed, and upset. He told me that he was HIV positive." John fell silent for a moment, and Sammy thought he could hear his voice pinch across the following words. "It was hard to take. I thought he would survive for a while. Two months later… he came down with AIDS.

"His health deteriorated rapidly. About two years ago, he got severely ill and never recovered. I was with him, holding his hand when he passed away. None of his family members was there." John nodded in thought. "I felt… so alone then. I had no one to share my feelings with, no one to call. I felt so alone."

Sammy swallowed the lump in his throat and took John's hand. "I'm sorry to hear that. I understand how difficult that is. That's very tragic."

Tears rolled down John's cheeks. He wiped them on his shoulder and pointed to the framed photo perched atop the piano. "That's Adam."

"He was a handsome man."

John sniffed. "It's difficult to find friends now. I tried. I have friends, but it feels like I can't connect with anyone, like my heart has hardened. I don't know. I don't feel comfortable with anyone anymore. I miss Adam."

"Yeah, but Adam will always be with you. I went through a similar experience. I lost someone very close to me. I lost two of my brothers. One brother died when he was a child before I was born. So I didn't know him. But the other, I knew well. He was my close friend. I was with him when he died. I went through… agony and suffering. I feel your pain."

"What happened?" murmured John into the space between them.

Sammy collected his thoughts before he began. "My brother and I were coming back from visiting our aunts one September evening, walking along the side streets that led to our small neighborhood. It was quiet, not a sound. I remember looking up to admire the clarity of the sky and the brightness of the stars.

"See, our neighborhood was isolated in a sense, so we had to walk down this narrow street to get there. It was the only one. Well, there had been protests earlier that day, and the army had been all over the place beating up people. All of a sudden, an Israeli military jeep turned the corner and came down that narrow street. It squealed to a stop just inches from us. We couldn't move; we were frozen.

"A couple of soldiers jumped out and started yelling for us to put our hands in the air. And we did. And then they beat us with clubs, very thick and heavy clubs. One of the soldiers hit my brother on the back of his head; my brother dropped. I screamed. The soldiers got back in their jeep and drove away.

"I… tried to wake him up. He was still alive, but he wouldn't open his eyes. I ran home, yelling for help. Family and neighbors came out running after me. We couldn't do anything to help him. I stayed next to him all night, watching him breathe, watching his chest go up and down, hoping that it would never stop. I begged him to wake up. But he never did. The next morning, he died. My mother was beside herself. She wept nonstop and loudly. All she could say was, 'They killed my son!' My father cried and called the soldiers criminals."

"Shit…" John muttered.

"My brother had been one of the brightest kids in our neighborhood. I was fourteen when that happened; he was twenty. We were very close. I went with him everywhere. He always encouraged me to go to school and promised that he would do his best to send me to college. But my brother was a day laborer in Israel. As humiliating as it was, that was his only option. He didn't make a lot of money and he worked long, hard hours. He was determined to send me to school." Sammy licked his suddenly dry lips and swirled his wine. "I felt so alone after he died. All hope was gone. I didn't want to live anymore." He glanced at John. "So, yeah, I know how it feels to lose someone dear to you."

Tears tracking down his face, John set aside his wine and embraced Sammy, clutching him to his chest. He kissed the top of his head and held him. "I'm so, so sorry. It must have been very hard for you," he whispered.

Sammy tried to keep his voice from trembling. "The same day he died, he was buried. He died in the morning, and a few hours later, everyone carried him to the mosque and then to the cemetery to be buried. It was the saddest day of my life. I couldn't do anything to help him, to protect him. I'm *still* angry. Why kill him? He didn't do anything. Every time I saw an army jeep, I became frightened. I saw my brother collapsing beside me again and again." He drew a long breath and, through pursed lips said, "It may sound selfish, but I'm glad I'm not there anymore. In Palestine. At times, I feel guilty living in comfort and peace while my family and friends remain in danger. I don't... I don't know how they manage to keep going." He stubbornly drew away. "We shouldn't keep talking about these things. It's depressing. See what happens when you ask me to talk? It's your turn."

John playfully, tenderly touched him. "No, I'm glad you're sharing with me. It shows me your other side. We can't keep these experiences locked away. We need to be honest."

Sammy considered his words before saying, "This whole week, I've been thinking of us, of our relationship. And I've been scared. There are so many differences between us—culturally, socially, even in the way we think. So I want to be careful with how we talk. Please don't misunderstand me, John. I like you so much. I'm just hesitant."

"About?"

"I'm not *out*. I can't be. But you are. You are out everywhere, at work, with your friends and family. I'm not out anywhere. John, I feel I am not out to myself sometimes. This idea of a relationship between two men is difficult for me to comprehend. I know it is there, and I feel it, but I can't accept it. Maybe because of my religion, maybe because of my culture, or maybe because of how I was raised. But I feel ashamed."

John chuckled. "Don't think too much about it."

Sammy looked at him abruptly, surprised.

"These things will take care of themselves. It doesn't matter to me if you are out or not. The issue is completely up to you."

"You say that now," replied Sammy, "but when we are together, that can be... uncomfortable for me."

"You think too much—"

The phone rang. John glanced at the phone before reluctantly answering it. "No, not now. I can't talk to you right now. I'll call later." He hung up.

Sammy watched him, taking the moment to pull himself out of the emotional reviewing of his traumatic memories. *Maybe it's somebody from his past?*

"Like I was saying," John continued. "You think too much."

Silence blossomed between them as each fell into his own thoughts. But it was not an uncomfortable quiet. Even as they thought, John grasped Sammy's hand and rubbed his thumb along the side of it.

And in that moment, Sammy knew that John wasn't just a passing affair.

Spurred by the intimate touches and the warmth of John's skin, Sammy struggled to keep his heart from racing. Maybe he didn't love John; maybe he just lusted for him. But when he looked at his handsome face, Sammy wanted to fall into his arms over and over again. He told himself to hide his emotions, to keep some part of him safe. But he knew that was impossible. When he was with John, he wanted time to stop.

John seemed to sense his mood shift because he gave a soft smile and then leaned in and kissed him. Though Sammy longed to be touched and held, the thoughts that tore through his mind were degrading and brought shame to him.

Wake up! You can't fall in love like this! What the hell are you doing having a relationship with a man?

Clearing his throat, Sammy gently pulled away. "It's getting late. I should leave. And you have a phone call to return."

"I don't have to call back tonight. That was my father. He just wanted to talk about work. I didn't think now was the time."

"Well, still, I should go—"

"No, no. I'll call him tomorrow. Besides, why do you have to go? You could stay the night."

"I don't have any work clothes."

John flashed a smile at him. "I could lend you a suit."

"Yeah, but I didn't tell Michael that I was staying overnight."

With a warm chuckle, John led Sammy to his bedroom and began dragging out suits for him to try on. The first one fit. John matched a tie and shirt with it. A few minutes later, Sammy begrudgingly called Michael to let him know that he was staying at John's that night.

"Uh, thanks for the suit," Sammy said, politely hanging it along the doorway.

"It looks good on you," replied John, stashing the other ensembles.

"I'll bring it back tomorrow night."

"Bring it back tomorrow night so I can see you again," John countered.

Sammy fidgeted. His inner thoughts raced as an onslaught of demoralizing words berated his consciousness.

"So, which side of the bed do you like?" joked John. "I prefer the middle."

"Well, maybe we'll both sleep in the middle."

Sammy self-consciously undressed and slid into bed where John waited for him. They bid each other goodnight with soft kisses and then fell still.

After several quiet minutes, John asked, "You asleep?"

"No, I'm awake."

"Nervous?"

"Yes."

"Why?"

"Because… this is my first time to be with a man overnight."

"Wait. Really?"

"I didn't even get to brush my teeth," Sammy said.

John chuckled. "I can fix that. Come on."

After giving Sammy a new toothbrush and privacy to brush his teeth, John returned to the room to wait for him. Feeling a little more relaxed, Sammy joined him in bed. Still, he couldn't sleep.

"Hey, I know what we could do to help us sleep…" John muttered, rolling into him.

CHAPTER 5

THE FOLLOWING MORNING, JOHN WOKE Sammy with his alarm. After turning it off, John lay beside him to study his profile in the dim light. He had never before felt so comfortable with someone, felt so complete. He allowed his satisfaction to erase the discomfort he had felt the previous night as Sammy had spoken about his home and past in Gaza.

Pushing aside the cognitive dissonance that lurked in the back of his mind, John got up.

Sammy joined him in the kitchen sometime later once the coffee had finished brewing, and they sat at the table and had breakfast together.

"I can't be late for work," Sammy murmured, minding the clock on the wall.

"I'll skip work today if you do," John replied with a charming smile. "Let's stay home. Find an excuse." Seeing the look on Sammy's face, he gently added, "We can call in sick."

"Or we can just go in late?" offered Sammy, peering at him from over his coffee mug.

And that's what they did. They spent the morning in bed, making love and talking. John intentionally did not bring up anything that would touch upon or even brush the topic of politics or religion.

Sammy went home after work to find Michael cooking dinner for them as usual. Ever appreciative, Sammy immediately jumped in to help with the inconsequential tasks of washing cutting boards and chopping vegetables.

"Well?" asked Michael. "How did it feel to stay overnight at a stranger's house?"

"It wasn't bad. Actually…" Sammy grinned slightly. "It was really exciting and enjoyable. It was a different feeling having someone sleep next to me in bed. And we spent the morning in bed too."

Michael laughed. "Oh yeah?"

Sammy nodded. "We went to work late." He sighed. "I feel different toward him. It's a strange feeling. I like him more than anybody I've ever liked. But there's a lot to think about. We're so different, but we're so compatible."

"It sounds scary being that vulnerable," admitted Michael.

"It is, but I can't stop now." Considering his roommate's sage words, Sammy said, "I never asked—How did you meet Joseph? I'm curious."

Michael shrugged. "A bathhouse."

"A bathhouse?"

His roommate chuckled. "Yeah, bathhouses aren't exactly known for being romantic. They're known for being, uh, seedy places. But yeah, the bathhouse."

"I'd like to hear more," Sammy encouraged.

"All right. Well, we were sitting by the jacuzzi, both naked. It's a bathhouse, right? We started chatting, and he asked if I wanted to go back to his room with him. He was attractive, so I went. The next thing I know, sixteen years had passed." He leaned against the counter and gazed wistfully out the window. "I miss him."

"Me too."

In an obvious attempt to change the subject, Michael grinned at Sammy. "So, tell me about John. What's he like?"

"Handsome. If there were ever a man for me, it would be him."

"Seems like you're ready for a relationship," Michael replied.

Sammy thought. "My real dream was to be married and have children."

"It doesn't have to be with a woman. You can adopt," offered Michael. Sammy frowned at him. "Could you feel for a woman what you do for John? What if you married a woman but still had feelings for a man? How would your wife feel? That would be deceptive, right?" Michael regarded him. "I'm sorry. I'm not trying to be harsh."

"You're right though," Sammy replied softly. "I thought about that myself. But... all my brothers and sisters are married—with children—except me and my youngest sister. My mother is looking for a wife for me. She had my sister write a letter, telling me that she was looking."

"Relationships are complicated," said Michael. "There is nothing simple about this situation. Think long and hard and don't make rash decisions." He sat back. "So, when are you going to see John again?"

"I'm sure it'll be soon. The truth is I can't wait to be with him again."

Michael chuckled warmly. "Oh, well, that's good. Maybe you should bring him over and introduce him to me sometime. I'll cook lunch for the three of us. On a Sunday. Or we can have a barbecue."

Sammy thought about the offer and then smiled. "Yeah, that sounds good—"

The house phone rang. When Michael made a move to retrieve it, Sammy waved for him to sit back down and answered. It was John. Sammy couldn't help the dumb smile on his face. It came naturally when he heard John's voice.

They briefly exchanged light-hearted chitchat before John laughed. "So, I don't think we should spend the night together in the middle of the week anymore."

"Oh. Why?" asked Sammy.

"Because I didn't sleep well at all. And then I had to work."

Relieved, Sammy chuckled. "I agree."

"Maybe just on the weekends?"

"Yeah, that'd probably be best," replied Sammy, pacing back and forth with the phone.

"Okay, I'll call you and let you know about this upcoming weekend."

"Okay, talk to you soon."

As soon as Sammy hung up the phone, Michael asked, "He wanting to see you this weekend?"

"Yeah. I think he wants me to spend the entire weekend with him."

"Well, why not? Do you have any other plans?"

"No." Sammy returned to the table. "But where is this leading?"

"You decide, Sammy."

There was a long moment of silence between them before Sammy said, "I think I'm going to write a letter to my parents. I haven't... written to them in a long time and feel like I need to communicate with them. I wish they had a phone."

"Feeling homesick?"

"I'm not sure," replied Sammy. "Maybe my deep connection with John is triggering it. I miss my home, my parents, my siblings. I miss the beach, the sea, eating fresh fish in the morning. I know my family wants to know everything about me, but I can't... I can't tell them about much of what is going on in my life."

"Like John," Michael offered.

Sammy nodded. "I can share a little bit with them, but then it feels like a superficial relationship. It's very confusing and frustrating." He sighed. "I don't know what I'm going to write about. I can't tell them about my work; they wouldn't understand." He floundered for a moment, thinking. "I'll just tell them that I miss them. It's been ten years since I've seen them. I... wonder how they look now." Sammy glanced at Michael. "I wonder how much I've changed."

"You're not that little boy on the beach next to the Mediterranean anymore," said Michael with a smile.

Sammy nodded and headed upstairs. Once he set the window in his bedroom ajar, he sat at his desk.

He began writing. And then scribbled the lines out and started again.

He began writing. And then crushed the paper and swept it to the floor.

He began writing. And then lay his head atop the fresh ink in despair.

He had no idea what to tell them, what to share. All that he could manage was that he was doing well. It felt so insincere, so distant.

After a good hour of struggling to pen anything coherent, Sammy went downstairs for water. Unsurprisingly, Michael was at the table completing a crossword puzzle and sipping a cup of decaffeinated tea.

"I meant to ask," Michael mused without looking up from his puzzle, "you like John, right?"

Sammy nodded.

"How's he make you feel? I mean, if you're willing to answer."

Sammy retrieved a glass of water. "Honestly, when it comes to John, I don't know what I'm thinking myself. I'm confused most of the time. I'd like to introduce him to you. Maybe next Sunday we can have him over?"

"That sounds nice," replied Michael.

"Do… you want to invite anyone else?"

"No."

Sammy studied him. "It's been two years since Joseph passed. I haven't seen you with anyone since."

"I go out sometimes."

"I meant romantically," Sammy corrected.

"I'm not up to that yet." Michael fidgeted with his pencil. "It's going to take some time. I don't feel I'm emotionally available yet. I'm out of circulation." He chuckled. "Even if I did go out, I wouldn't know how to approach anyone, what to talk about, how to start a relationship. It's different now. Besides, I'm not young anymore. I'm fifty-seven."

"You're too hard on yourself. I'm sure you'll find someone."

"Oh, no. That's not what I meant. I meant that it's too late for me."

Sammy scoffed. "It's never too late."

"Where to start, where to go… I don't like bars. People my age don't go to bars. Dancing? No… I wouldn't do that. That's not my scene."

"Just… promise you won't give up," pushed Sammy, meeting his gaze.

Michael glanced down at his puzzle. "I'll think about it."

CHAPTER 6

SAMMY AND JOHN STAYED IN touch throughout the week, talking at least once a day via phone. The conversations furthered their forming connection and made Sammy feel as though he better understood John and his routine. There was no shortage of subjects and no lack of words between them. In Sammy's eyes, life began to look brighter as his inhibitions and resistance to being involved in such a relationship weakened. He smiled more. Even his coworkers noticed the change and began to engage with him.

Sammy invited John to dinner at his and Michael's home on Sunday, and without hesitation, John accepted. Of course, when Sunday arrived, Sammy was sick with anxiety and frantically cleaned to make the abode presentable. He and Michael worked together to make salads and Middle Eastern-style baba ghanoush and hummus.

"What time is he supposed to arrive?" asked Michael, mixing a salad.

"I told him around 4:00."

Michael checked the clock over his shoulder. "It's only 3:15."

"I realize that," Sammy snapped. He passed his roommate an apologetic look. "Sorry. I just want everything to be perfect."

Michael chuckled. "Don't worry so much. The place is clean. You're handsome. Let's put this in the fridge and then have a beer."

Once the kitchen was tidy, they grabbed drinks and sat out on the back porch.

"I gave John specific directions on how to get here. I hope he doesn't get lost, but if he does, he has a cell phone in his car. He can call."

"Oh, does he?" mused Michael.

"I'm thinking of getting one. They're becoming more affordable these days." Sammy bounced his foot against the side of the chair. He glanced at Michael, who passed him an amused look, and then jumped up and started to pace the yard. Within minutes, he was pulling weeds, picking up leaves, and checking every flower.

"Michael," Sammy called. "The petunias are doing well this year. Look at these colors. Oh, and so are the roses!"

Michael joined him, and they admired the blooms together. "The roses were Joseph's favorite, especially that color. What an unusual color; it's almost purple." He sighed. "Taking care of the garden brought him great joy. I miss him terribly."

The phone rang from within the house, and Sammy trotted inside to answer it. It was John.

"Uh, I think my car overheated," he explained breathlessly. "It stalled. But don't worry. I'm not too far from your house. I'm coming over."

"Don't be silly. I'll come get you," replied Sammy, already turning to search for his keys.

"No, a gentleman stopped to help me. He volunteered to drive me to you. Said he was going in that direction anyhow. I, uh, called a tow truck already, but it's going to be a while. I'll need a ride back home later though."

"Yeah, of course. I can do that."

"Great. Okay, see you soon!"

John and the gentleman arrived a few minutes later. Sammy met them in the driveway.

"I have no idea what that was about!" exclaimed John, grinning at Sammy. He motioned to the balding driver who joined them. "This fellow here is Jim. This is my friend Sammy."

Jim was in his mid-fifties and boasted a small amount of salt-and-pepper hair on the sides of his head. He was tall with shockingly blue eyes and a light complexion.

Sammy shook his hand in greeting. "Thank you for helping John out. Please, come in. Would you care for a beer?"

Jim smiled broadly. "Yeah, that sounds good. Thank you!"

Sammy led them through the house to the back porch where Michael still sipped on his own beverage. Introductions were short.

"What an amazing garden," Jim remarked, marveling at the foliage. "Did you do it all yourself?"

Michael beamed first at Jim and then at John. "Oh yes, Sammy and I work in it often."

They kept up small talk for a few minutes before Jim politely excused himself and left. Sammy saw Michael turn to John, a smile on his lips.

"I've heard so much about you. I've been looking forward to meeting you," said his roommate.

"I feel as if I already know you," John laughed.

"Well, hey, let's go check out your car real quick. Maybe before the tow truck gets there?" Michael offered.

"It's getting late. We should start cooking," Sammy replied.

Michael threw him a look. "It'll be fine. If it doesn't start, then we'll just come back." He motioned to John and led him to the garage.

Climbing into Michael's Toyota, John remarked, "Your car is so clean. I feel ashamed to show you mine."

Michael seemed amused as he buckled in. "I take it once a week to have it cleaned. Just did it this morning." He glanced at John who had yet to draw his seatbelt across his shoulder.

"I'm fine," John said. When Michael gave him a look, he added, "I know I should, but I hate feeling trapped."

"It's required by law now," Michael replied, shifting gears to back out of the driveway. "But really it's for your safety."

John reluctantly pulled on the seatbelt. He tried not to let the silence that ensued ruffle him, but it was difficult to stay calm. Michael knew Sammy intimately. John just had to figure out how to access that information.

After a few minutes, John pointed up ahead. "That's it. The champaign-colored Chevrolet. You know, the one that hasn't seen a car wash in a few years."

Chuckling, Michael pulled onto the shoulder and put his flashers on. As John scurried over to his car, Michael retrieved a toolbox from his trunk. Together, they began solving the mystery as to why John's car had so suddenly halted.

"So… how long have you known Sammy?" John eventually asked.

"Since he was fourteen," Michael replied, peering into the innards of the engine. "When we were in Gaza."

"In Gaza? You? How?"

"Me and Joseph used to work for the UNRWA—the United Nations Relief and Works Agency for Palestine Refugees."

"That's a name!" chuckled John. "And Joseph? He was your partner, right?"

Michael glanced at him. "Yeah, he died of AIDs two years ago."

John's mouth went dry. He swallowed. "I lost a close friend of mine to AIDs two years ago. I'm… really sorry to hear that. The government's not doing much about the pandemic. We need a vaccine."

"The government's started to pay more attention now." Michael stood back, his brows furrowed as he studied the engine. "The gay community is organizing and becoming more aware of safe sex practices. So, we've got that going for us."

"True." John considered how best to ask his next question. "You've known Sammy for a long time. I'm sure you know him well. I… have a question; I hope it's not too sensitive to ask."

Michael took his scrutinizing gaze from the engine and met John's eyes. "Shoot."

"Often, Sammy seems aloof, sad. I sometimes have a hard time understanding him. Do you know… if that, uh, is because of me or something I've done?"

"Uh, no. It's not you. Sammy has led a difficult life. Growing up in Gaza isn't easy. Life there is hard and violent." Michael passed him a smile. "Give him some time." He motioned to the car. "As we were talking, I think I know what's wrong with it."

When they returned, John excitedly declared the car mobile and so canceled the tow truck. Although anxious while they were gone, Sammy could discern a new sense of ease between Michael and John and decided it had been good to let them chat alone.

Dinner was a pleasant affair with much laughter and conversation. There was great chemistry between the three, and Michael and John fed off each other's sense of humor. Sammy also tried his hand at American jokes but found that his accent marred much of the delivery. Still, he greatly enjoyed himself.

Shortly before 9:00, John excused himself. He graciously thanked Michael before allowing Sammy to walk him to his car. There he kissed Sammy hard, holding him with fondness. Sammy didn't resist but feared what the neighbors might say. John tapped his face. "I'll talk to you tomorrow."

He slid into the car, backed out of the driveway, gave a small wave, and then left.

Sammy returned to the kitchen to help Michael clean up. "That went well," he said, smiling. "It was nice of you to fix John's car."

Michael chuckled. "He's a nice boy. I like him. He's funny, good-looking." He nudged Sammy. "Is he good in bed?"

Sammy gaped in mock umbrage, his face burning, and then smiled. "Yes, very good."

Despite the pleasant atmosphere of the evening, Sammy had a hard time sleeping that night. The faces of his family flashed in his mind's eye, and once more, he began composing a letter in his head, trying to explain to his parents how much he missed them. He missed sitting on the floor of the house with his siblings. He missed his mother's generous hugs and warm words of encouragement…

Thinking of his mother reminded him of her current challenge—to find him a wife.

Yes, he would go back someday, but he wouldn't be marrying.

Not to a woman.

Coming to America had been a shock to him. He had managed to adjust and assimilate some, but the differences remained tremendous. He had never accepted the fact that he was gay, but he was beginning to come around to the idea. He knew his uncertainties and insecurities made it difficult for him to talk to John. But much of it was influenced by the oppression and violence that had plagued his young life.

Religion had also acted as a major influence in his upbringing. Like Christianity, Islam condemned homosexuality and often dictated harsh punishment for its practice. It was absolutely a taboo. His family had never talked about the subject as it was shameful. It was not Islamic; he couldn't get rid of it easily.

In the morning Sammy and Michael met at the kitchen table over a cup of coffee.

"Don't forget," said Michael, "next Sunday we have the neighborhood picnic."

"Are we going?"

"It's a good idea," replied Michael. "I would like to meet the people in the neighborhood. The subdivision is going to close the street leading to our house. The picnic is going to be at the park across the street." He grinned. "I've never been, but I've seen it happen every year. And this year, I want to go."

Sammy agreed, "Then we'll go Sunday."

CHAPTER 7

Over the following week, Sammy didn't see John and so resorted to calling him multiple times throughout each day. Their evening conversations tended to be long, and Sammy often fell asleep listening to John's calming voice.

Midway through the week, John shared that he was going out of town that weekend to visit his mother in New York. Disappointed but understanding, Sammy wished him a safe trip.

Saturday morning found Sammy and Michael in the yard as usual, picking weeds, trimming bushes, and cutting the grass. It was a beautiful summer day.

"I'm thinking of going out tonight," Sammy eventually announced.

"Yeah?"

"Maybe I'll go to the clubs to dance. I don't know." Sensing Michael's gaze on him, Sammy continued. "I'm happy with John. But I still have these… internal conversations with myself. It's so depressing. Part of me loves to be in a relationship. But the other part of me can't imagine being with a man."

"Maybe you and I need to sit and have a conversation. In my opinion, you might need to see a therapist. The way you view relationships isn't healthy."

Sammy fidgeted uncomfortably. He knew Michael was right. Sammy resented the fact that he was gay and looked for every opportunity to reject it. But the harder he fought, the more obvious it became. Still, he was grateful for Michael and wanted to show his appreciation. "What time is the picnic tomorrow?"

"It starts around 11:00."

"Oh, that's good. That gives us time to sleep in tomorrow. How about we go out to eat tonight? Just the two of us?"

Michael beamed. "Hey, now that's a good idea! We haven't been out in a while."

"How about a restaurant in Boystown? I can take you where I took John. The food was really good."

They went out that night and had a pleasant time. They talked about John, Joseph, themselves, and the food. When it grew late, Michael decided to head home, but Sammy chose to visit a club, marching directly to the dance floor. He didn't drink much, as he had never been the cruising type. Instead, he just danced.

That night, many men tried to pick him up. Some started conversations with him, but Sammy talked briefly and then kept dancing. There were many nice-looking men available, but Sammy found himself drawn to no one. As the evening wore on, he began wishing John was dancing with him.

Shortly after 1:00, a man approached Sammy and asked if he would like to join him for a drink. When the admirer didn't pick up on Sammy's nonverbal communication and insisted that he come home with him, Sammy evenly said, "No, I'm already in a relationship."

Watching the man sidle back through the crowd, Sammy wondered what had possessed him to say such a thing. That he was already in a relationship with someone…

After that, he left in a hurry, fully uncomfortable with what he had spoken aloud. The internal degradation that he had come to expect on the way home blared in his head like usual. He was both excited to have admitted his status aloud and horrified.

Once home, he went to the answering machine to check for any messages. He was relieved to find one from John telling him that he missed him and that he wished he was also in New York. John left a phone number, which Sammy eagerly wrote down intending to call the next day.

The following morning, he and John had a lengthy phone conversation, but Sammy didn't bring up the previous night's club experience. It made him feel too self-conscious.

A few minutes before 11:00, he and Michael headed out for the neighborhood picnic. Even from a distance, they could hear the noise of people, the screaming and laughter of children, and the barking of excited dogs. The delicious aroma of food floated on the wind. They arrived at the park to find a multitude of picnickers. Though they superficially knew their immediate neighbors, most of the people present were strangers.

Sammy looked about at the happy families and married couples and leaned into Michael. "What are we doing here? We're the only gays here."

Michael chuckled. "Yes, Sammy, this is called a society."

"Yeah, but we don't know anyone here."

"Be patient," chided Michael. "Let's walk around and mingle."

Across the park, Sammy spotted a group of teenagers playing volleyball and chasing one another.

Michael followed his gaze. "I wonder how many of them are gay." He motioned to the other families present. "I wonder how many gay people are in our neighborhood."

"Two," supplied Sammy. "You and me."

"Naw. Look at all these teens. I doubt all of them are straight. Could you imagine how much suffering they go through, and how much pretense they have to keep up to satisfy the people around them? It must be hard on these kids to grow up in a community and with family who don't accept them for what they are." He lowered his voice. "Suicide rates among teenage gay boys are much higher than the national average."

"I grew up in a society that was harder than this one. I know what it is to pretend, and I know what it is to suffer. I contemplated suicide a few times when I was a teenager. I was taught from childhood not to accept my sexuality. I was taught to be ashamed of it. I still am…" Sammy looked about uncomfortably and kept his voice low. "Most parents love their children only if the children fulfill the expectations of their parents, which is basically to be heterosexual. Unconditional love is rare to find. I'm not even sure it exists."

"Oh! Look!" exclaimed Michael, pointing. "Isn't that Jim, the guy who brought John over last weekend?"

"Oh, it is." Sammy watched him and the young woman he was with. "His wife's pretty. Must be his second. What do you think?"

"I agree. I think they have a kid running around here. Oh, Jim's coming over. At least we know someone!" Michael enthusiastically greeted Jim, who recognized them, and introduced them to his daughter, Jessica.

"You must have married very young," remarked Sammy without any type of filtering.

Jim chuckled good-naturedly. "I did. Jessica's my only daughter," he pointed across the park, "and the little one in red over there is my grandson. His name is Jordan."

"You have a beautiful son, Jessica," said Michael.

"Oh, thank you," grinned Jessica, "but he drives me crazy. He wants to be everywhere all the time. It's the terrible twos. Do you live nearby?"

"Our house is a block and a half from here," Michael replied.

"Your father helped my friend last weekend when his car broke down outside the subdivision," added Sammy.

Jessica settled her curious gaze on Sammy. "Where are you from? You have an accent."

Sammy bristled but hid his discomfort. The question always put him on edge. "I am Palestinian."

"Oh, Palestinian," she replied warmly. "You're the first I've ever met. You look different."

"What do you mean?" probed Sammy.

"Just that you look different. You're a nice-looking man."

"Thank you, but many Palestinian men are good-looking. You haven't met any. You said I am the first one."

"Oh, I meant from what I've seen on TV," Jessica quickly corrected.

Despite Michael's gentle nudges, Sammy continued. "What you see on TV is not an accurate picture of Palestinians at all. It is pure propaganda. It's a deliberate distortion of their image."

Jessica glanced at her father who gently intervened. "So, Sammy, what brought you to America?"

"I came here to go to school, and then I stayed. I was offered a good job," Sammy replied.

"Man, what a beautiful day!" Michael exclaimed. "This is my first time at the neighborhood picnic. Usually, I'm too busy to attend. It's so nice to meet everyone. I'm surprised, Jim, that we haven't seen you around before."

"Oh, I live a few blocks from here, in a court. We're not out very often. Probably just missed each other. You have a lovely house, Michael, especially your backyard." To Jessica, he said, "Their garden is beautiful. The flowers are well taken care of. You should see it."

"It's our hobby," Michael replied. "I enjoy doing yard work, and Sammy helps."

"I enjoy working in the yard too, but my backyard isn't nearly as pretty as yours. I grow vegetables—tomatoes, cucumbers, you know the sort. We have plenty. I'll have to bring you some. Sometimes we don't know what to do with them all, especially the zucchini and tomatoes."

As Michael led the way in small talk, Sammy observed the happy families and inserted appropriate remarks. Eventually, Jessica collected little Jordan. Declaring the toddler was too tired to continue, she and Jim excused themselves from the festivities.

Michael leaned into Sammy and whispered, "You *have* to calm down. You tend to get too emotional when any issue related to Palestine is brought up. People will stop listening to you."

John came back from New York. Sammy met him for dinner a few times over the following week and stayed overnight at his apartment.

On Friday, when Sammy came home from work, he found a box of vegetables in the kitchen that Jim had dropped off. "That was nice of him," Sammy remarked, perusing the zucchini and tomatoes.

"It really was," replied Michael who was already cooking dinner. "I talked with him for a while this afternoon on the phone. Turns out he lives alone with his daughter and her son. He was divorced a while ago. His daughter and grandson moved in a little over a year ago. Jim was telling me that it was quite the adjustment. He had a hard time learning to live with a child again."

"Divorced, huh?" mused Sammy.

"Yeah." Michael sighed. "But it seems like Jim's interested in getting to know us. He's a friendly person."

"Do you think he's gay?" asked Sammy.

"Anything is possible, but he doesn't seem like it. He's probably not. With the way he lives, I doubt it very much. But you never know." He smiled. "I shouldn't say that. I think stereotyping for any situation or any group of people is wrong. I guess we'll learn in time. So, tell me about you and John! What's going on?"

"It's good. I talked with him today. I'll see him tomorrow night. We're going out for dinner, and he'll probably invite me to stay the night, to which I will not say no."

Michael passed him a warm grin as the phone rang. Since his roommate was busy cutting the new assortment of vegetables, Sammy answered. It was John.

"Hey, I was just talking about you," Sammy said.

John chuckled uncomfortably. "Yeah? Um, well, I was actually calling because I need to cancel tomorrow's dinner."

"Did something happen?" asked Sammy.

"Yeah, something's come up. I have to go see my father."

Sammy couldn't hide his disappointment. "Oh."

"I'll talk with you soon."

"Yeah, bye."

The moment he hung up, Sammy's doubts and insecurities rushed to the surface, pushing him to think of worst-case scenarios.

"What happened?" asked Michael.

"He, uh, had to cancel dinner tomorrow night. He has to see his father."

"You and I could go out if you'd like. But I can't go to the same places you go to. I don't like noisy spots."

"Yeah…" Sammy considered the offer. "We could visit a piano bar. There's one on Halsted Street."

Michael agreed.

"And I'll cook tomorrow. How about fish? Are you okay with that?"

"Sounds great."

Saturday morning, Jim called to borrow Michael's ladder so he could clip the high branches that covered his bedroom window. Sammy offered to help, but Jim insisted that he could do it himself. When Jim came to collect the ladder, they stood in the garden and discussed gardening and Jessica and her son. That was how Sammy learned that Jim was home alone.

"It feels good to be alone sometimes," Jim replied.

"Tonight, Sammy is cooking dinner. He's cooking fish, very likely Palestinian-style. Would you care to join us?"

Surprise flashed across Jim's face. "Oh, that would be wonderful. Yes, I'd like that very much."

That afternoon as Sammy prepped everything, he asked Michael, "Should we pretend in front of him?"

"What do you mean?"

"Do we have to pretend that we're straight? Or maybe we should avoid the subject completely."

Michael sighed. "Don't think about it. Just be comfortable and be yourself. Don't pretend anything that you're not."

"But what if he's a homophobe?"

"Don't worry. He will eat and leave. He seems like a nice man, very socially engaging. He won't say anything."

Jim arrived punctually. The food was almost ready. Having learned how to cook fish from his mother, Sammy took pride in his skills and so left the vegetables and saffron rice to Michael.

"Oh, it smells good," Jim uttered, passing his eyes over the simmering pans.

They had cocktails just before dinner and kept to light conversation about the same issues—the garden, the neighborhood, the weather, and a little bit about the politics of the day. When Sammy declared supper ready, they gathered around the table.

"I like the way you cooked the fish, Sammy," said Jim. "It's very unique, very different."

"Thank you," replied Sammy with a pleased smile. "It's my mother's recipe."

"Where is the rest of your family, Sammy? Do you have family in America?"

"The only family I have in America is Michael. Everyone else lives in the Gaza Strip."

Jim's brows rose in surprise. "Gaza! What a place to live in. I hear about it and see it on the news often. It looks terrible, dangerous."

"Yes, it can be dangerous. People have no safety in their homes."

"You don't look like them. You're a handsome man," offered Jim.

Minding his conversation with Michael from the previous weekend, Sammy cautiously replied, "Thank you, Jim, but there are many handsome Palestinian men, just most in the West don't see them."

"That's true," Jim acquiesced. "Well, you should be proud of yourself. You've done well. You succeeded, Sammy." He motioned between Sammy and Michael. "How did you two meet?"

Sammy glanced at Michael, letting him decide how to answer the difficult question.

Michael chuckled. "Well, it's a long story. Maybe sometime we'll sit down and tell you about it."

"Right, right," Jim graciously agreed.

"Your daughter, Jessica, does she work?"

"She's going to school right now. She's a single mother, and that can be difficult. That's why she's living with me. Hopefully, she'll finish school soon and find a job and move out. When she first had the baby, she lived with her mother, but her mother's boyfriend couldn't take it and forced her to leave. I'm not going to let my daughter depend on welfare. So the only solution was for her to move in with me."

Forgetting to practice filtering his responses and questions, Sammy asked, "What about the father? Jordan's father? What about his responsibilities?"

"Oh, the father has nothing to do with Jordan. Jessica doesn't love him anymore. She just wanted to have the baby."

Though Sammy nodded in understanding, he couldn't comprehend what Jim had just said. Back in Gaza, it was culturally and religiously unimaginable for a woman to have a child without being married. It was a crime.

The rest of the meal was eaten in a comfortable mixture of silence and tempered conversation. When Sammy offered coffee, Jim gladly accepted a mug of decaf.

"Yeah, it's nice having my daughter and grandson with me, but they definitely inhibit me. I'm not as free as I used to be. I used to have friends over for dinner. I can't do that anymore."

"Oh? Why not?" asked Michael, clearing dishes from the table.

"Eh, I don't think my daughter would like that," Jim replied. "Whenever I invite friends over, she takes her son and leaves and only comes back once they're gone. She's not comfortable with my choice of friends. At times, I feel she's not even comfortable with me, but I'm sure she will mature and understand that life isn't black and white."

Sammy exchanged furtive glances with Michael.

"But I do still get together with my friends. As a matter of fact, next month, it's my turn to entertain, and I've already made reservations at a restaurant for, like, twenty people."

"Twenty people?" gasped Michael. "That's so many!"

"It's a social club I belong to. It's my only social outlet, really. I'd like to invite you and Sammy. That'll make it twenty-two."

"Well, tell us when and where, and we'll check our calendar. We appreciate your invitation."

As Michael and Jim continued to talk, Sammy allowed his mind to wander to John. And he worried. What had happened that he had had to cancel dinner plans? Had his father said something? Was he okay? Maybe his father was sick.

John changed lanes, his mind preoccupied. What was so important that his father wanted to see him in person? Maybe he was sick. The first thing that came to mind was cancer. Despite the vast differences in opinions and personalities between him and his father, he loved him dearly.

Once at his father's house, John entered unannounced; the door was unlocked like usual. He found his father sitting in a comfortable recliner watching television. Linda, his father's girlfriend, warmly greeted him with hugs and kisses.

John leaned in and kissed the top of his father's head. "I'm here. Is everything okay?"

His father muted the television. "No, it's not. We need to talk." He sat up in the chair and watched as John seated himself nearby on the couch. "It's about that Palestinian boy."

"What about him?" John asked lowly.

"You need to stop seeing him."

John flushed, his eyes cutting to Linda, who had evidently shared with his father information that John had told her in private.

His father continued. "You being anywhere near him is completely unacceptable. It's not safe. You don't know anything about this guy. He could be a terrorist, and you wouldn't even know."

"It's *you* who doesn't know *him*," John shakily argued. "You're making these accusations but have never met him."

"They're not accusations," his father replied. "They're facts. Read the newspapers, watch the news. Evidence of the type of people they are is everywhere."

"You don't…" John stood, fists balled. "You don't know what you're talking about." He stormed out.

CHAPTER 8

SAMMY PACED HIS ROOM, WONDERING if he should call John. He picked up the phone several times and then returned it to its cradle, second-guessing himself. If it was important, John would call. Eventually though, Sammy couldn't resist and so reluctantly made the call.

"Hey."

"Hey, John. How was the visit with your father?" asked Sammy tensely.

"It was okay."

Sensing that he didn't want to talk about it, Sammy asked, "When do you want to meet this week?"

"I'm not sure. I have so many things going on." He sounded distant, uninterested.

"Is… something wrong? Is your father okay?"

"Yeah, he's fine."

"You don't sound like he's fine. Did something happen? Tell me."

"No, no. Everything's fine. I'll explain everything when I next see you."

"It's up to you, John," said Sammy.

"We could go after work to get a drink," John offered half-heartedly.

"No, I'd rather meet at a coffee shop."

So, they agreed to meet at the café on Halstead Street at 7:00 on Monday. Once Sammy hung up, he stayed by the phone for a long moment, his heart hammering. Something was wrong; he could sense it and hear it in John's voice. Something had happened. But what?

That evening, he went to open-mic night at the piano bar with Michael. Though surrounded by distractions, Sammy remained preoccupied with his conversation with John. That night, he had nightmares of explosions, fires, and gunshots, occasionally crying out in fear or alarm. Michael woke him calmly and brought him water and soft words. Sammy was too tired to be ashamed or embarrassed.

Monday, he and John met at the agreed-upon coffee shop. After ordering their espressos, they exchanged niceties, but Sammy remained aloof and worried, searching John for signs of impending trouble. Unable to bear it anymore, he finally asked softly, "What happened? Is everything okay with your father?"

"Yeah, he's… fine." John glanced at him. "Do you belong to any organizations?"

That was a weird question. "What do you mean?"

"Any social groups?"

"Like professional organizations?"

"No, I don't mean that." John fidgeted. "I mean other kinds of organizations. Any that maybe you joined before coming to the States?"

"What?"

John fiddled with his cup, sipped it, and then looked at Sammy. "Like any terrorist organizations?"

Sammy gaped at him, his eyes wide. A flurry of emotions rushed through him as he tried to process what John had just asked him. He fought to keep his voice even. "You are… the last person in the world who I thought would ask me that question." Sammy pursed his lips. "No, to answer your question."

John nodded.

Seething, Sammy sat back. "It's unfortunate you don't know what happened to us Palestinians. You've based your opinions on distorted, propagandist media and stories. We're a peaceful people who have been victimized and labeled terrorists." Sammy ran a thumb around the lip of his cup. "We were expelled from our homes, towns, and villages in a vicious campaign by Israeli forces. It was an ethnic cleansing.

"I don't think you know, John, that hundreds of thousands of Palestinians were expelled from their homes to become refugees in the surrounding countries. They weren't allowed to go back home by the Israeli government. Did you know that's called the Palestinian Catastrophe?"

Sammy regarded John who remained focused on the table between them.

"And now, we're called terrorists. Read up on our history. What I'm saying are not accusations; they are facts." Sammy took a breath to calm himself. "You're just like the rest of them. Judging and labeling. It's so easy to do. I'm sorry. I'm going to miss you, but I don't think we should continue seeing each other." Sammy stood. "Good luck, John."

"Sammy, wait." John grabbed his arm. "Wait, wait. I want to talk. You can't just leave because I asked a question."

"I am *beyond* hurt," Sammy fumed, his hands cold with adrenaline. "I'm devastated. And I'm leaving."

"Wait, wait, wait. Sammy. Wait, I'm sorry. It came out wrong. I'm trying to understand. I have so many… questions. You probably do too. Can we sit and talk like rational human beings?"

Sammy swallowed hard and returned to his seat. "You have more questions?"

John touched his hand. "Calm down. Please. This isn't about you or me. It's about the both of us."

Sammy worked to calm his breathing.

Still holding his hand, John said softly, "I read the newspaper often and see stories about Palestinian suicide bombers exploding buses, killing innocent people indiscriminately. Don't take anything personally. It's news and these are the facts. Israeli civilians are being killed by Palestinian terrorists." He met Sammy's eyes. "I get very angry about that."

"What those people do is unacceptable. I'm against all forms of violence. I get angry when Israeli soldiers kill innocent Palestinian people, and I get angry when Palestinians kill Israelis. This crazy behavior must stop—from both sides. But Israel has the upper hand."

John responded evenly. "Sammy, I'm… hurting as well. I realize how painful this is for you. I'm trying to understand."

Sammy glanced at his hand which was still covered by John's and then withdrew. Looking deeply into John's eyes, he said, "I hope one day you will understand. I'm leaving." In a hurry, Sammy left the coffee shop.

The hurt that threatened to swallow him whole was all-consuming. The conflict between Palestine and Israel wasn't new; neither were the difficulties that came with navigating intercultural relationships. But he hadn't expected this from John.

Sammy told himself to be strong, to stay the course. People in America were all the same—brainwashed. They couldn't think for themselves. He wasn't going to deny his heritage, his religion because of other people's ignorance or prejudice. Maybe the time to make a decision about their relationship had finally arrived.

Sammy drove home with tears in his eyes and a shattered heart. He had known prejudice and hatred; he understood both well. But perhaps he was too sensitive. Maybe John hadn't meant it the way he had, but it had still happened.

He pondered on what could have made John bring up such an outlandish topic. What had forced this sudden change? This sudden distrust?

A small piece of Sammy felt validated, as he had worried from the beginning that their differences in upbringing might complicate their relationship. And he had been right! But for the most part, he was heartbroken and felt that being born in Palestine was a curse. No matter where he went, hatred, suspicion, and ignorance followed him. He had been denied the right to be himself in Gaza, and now, in the United States, he was being forced to live a lie once again.

He arrived home, distraught, and went directly to his room. The answering machine flashed, revealing one waiting message. It was John.

"Sammy, I'm sorry if I hurt you. You misunderstood me. Please call me. I want to talk to you and clarify some issues."

Sammy started to call him back but hung up and instead went downstairs to find Michael at the table completing a crossword puzzle. He sat heavily across from his wise roommate. "John and I are no longer together."

"What? Why?" asked Michael, setting down his puzzle.

"I just broke us up. He asked me... if I was a member of a terrorist organization."

"He what?"

Sammy nodded, his eyes prickling. "Can you believe that? I was… so offended."

"That doesn't sound like him. Why would he ask that?" Michael gazed grimly at him. "I know how you must feel. What he asked is not acceptable. That was an ignorant and insensitive question. I'm sorry this happened. Be proud of yourself, and don't worry about him."

Wiping his eyes, Sammy said, "But he called and left a message, telling me I misunderstood. He wants me to call him back." He shook his head. "But I'm not going to. But…" He looked at Michael. "Why would he ask me that?"

Michael regarded him for a long moment and then said, "You have your suspicions, don't you?"

Sammy nodded. "Yeah, his father."

"I would call him. Not right now. But later, when you're calmer. Maybe tomorrow."

"Yeah…"

There was a stretch of silence between them before Michael asked, "By the way, are you going to Jim's party?"

"I'm not sure. Are you?"

"I would feel more comfortable if you went with me," replied Michael.

"Yeah, I'll come then." He tried to smile. "Maybe he's trying to match us up with some of his lady friends."

"Well, it's a way to enlarge our circle of friends. We haven't met any new people in a while."

That night, Sammy got very little sleep. He wrestled with how he should approach John and with what he was going to say. But his heart kept breaking as he struggled to face the fact that he had thought he had met the man of his dreams, somebody who actually loved him unconditionally. And now he was gone.

CHAPTER 9

After struggling to piece together a coherent conversation for most of the following day, Sammy finally called John. They agreed to meet at the same coffee shop on Halstead Street at 7:30 that evening.

They sat at the same table and ordered the same drinks. But there were no smiles, no warm conversation. The air was tense.

"Let's… communicate calmly, rationally," began John, holding his glass. "Why did you storm away? You left me there, alone. I was trying to explain to you my thoughts, and you just walked away. I'm serious about you, Sammy. You aren't a passing person in my life. So, for you to ignore me… hurt."

"What happened between you and your father? You didn't ask these questions before. Something happened, and I don't understand. Please tell me," replied Sammy. "I might feel more comfortable if you do. It'll help me understand."

"Uh, right." John thought for a moment. "Yeah, I visited my father that night I canceled. I had mentioned you to Linda, his girlfriend, and… she told him about us." He held his gaze. "So, my father starts asking questions about you. I didn't know how to answer them. He asked me if you belonged to a terrorist organization, if you're some sort of militant."

John gazed at the perspiration on his glass.

"When I was a kid, I heard so much about bloodshed and war. Palestinians—I tell you the truth, I never understood. But I never had a favorable image of them. I hated all of them… until I met you. You gave me a different picture of what a Palestinian is."

Sammy fought to stay calm, but he was disgusted. "I wonder if your father has ever met a Palestinian. I doubt it very much. He hates us from a distance. He hates us without knowing us. And you've been taught to hate us too."

"Sammy—"

"Now I understand your questions. The distance. You want answers, John? I will give you answers. No, I don't belong to a terrorist organization. And no, I'm not a militant." Sammy pushed his chair away. "We've had good times. And I thank you for those good times. Maybe someday you'll understand and know the facts about Palestinians and about the whole conflict. I don't know about your father… Maybe he's a hopeless case. Maybe he won't ever understand, though I hope he will. But someday, you'll get it." He stood. "I don't think we should see each other again. I don't think it's wise to even talk on the phone."

"Come on, Sammy," said John. "I just want to talk. If you can't bear to be near me, at least talk with me on the phone. I know you're hurting. I'm sorry I hurt you. But I really want you to know I have no hatred for you. It's the complete opposite. I like you. You know that. But please… let's keep talking. At least as friends, yeah?"

Sammy studied him for a long moment. "Fine, just as friends."

John smiled, relieved, but Sammy didn't return the gesture.

"So, what are you doing next weekend?"

"I'm going to a party."

"By yourself?"

"No, with Michael. Do you remember Jim, the guy who picked you up and drove you to my house when your car broke down? He's throwing a party."

"Oh… well, that sounds like fun."

"Yeah…"

They continued to chat over their drinks for the next hour, talking about different superficial issues. Sammy didn't actually want to leave. He feared that would be the last time he would ever see John. Though the tension between them eased some, it remained present. Finally, though, prompted by the encroaching night, Sammy explained, "I have a long drive ahead of me. We'll talk again… someday."

"Yes, I'll call you. I'll call you for sure," John assured him.

The drive home was a sad one. Sammy admitted he still loved John but knew that their relationship couldn't continue. They would never be able to resolve the conflict that had wedged into their unusual relationship. It was bigger than them.

Still, Sammy fantasized about John's hands and his strong shoulders and how his voice made Sammy feel loved. The way he talked, the way he moved—Sammy liked everything about him. Which made the realization of their fractured love that much more painful.

"So," called Michael from the kitchen when he got home. "Have a good day? Oh, did you meet John?"

"Yes, I did. We agreed to keep talking, but I know he's not for me, Michael. I know that now."

"What changed him? Did he say?"

"His father. His father basically told him that we're enemies. We're not supposed to be together." Sammy frowned. "It's like John *needs* his approval. No, he's not for me. I don't need anyone's approval but my own." He fell into thought. Sensing Michael's gaze on him, he said lowly, "But that's going to be hard because… I think I'm in love with him."

Michael smiled. "I know that, Sammy. I can see it in your eyes. As they say though, time heals all wounds. It's going to take *time*. Just like new clouds that take the place of old ones, new love can also take the place of old love. Maybe you need to go out and meet more people."

Sammy scoffed. "I'll meet more people—especially at Jim's party. He'll have lots of old married couples there. And the conversation is going to be about sports, hunting and fishing, their children and grandchildren… and they'll show everyone their kids."

Michael chuckled. "Well, Jim came by today and brought more vegetables. I'm going to use them tomorrow, so don't eat out then. I went ahead and told him that we're coming to his party."

"He seems nice. But I don't see anything in common between us."

"Well," said Michael, "we don't know him very well. It's difficult to judge. He has some interesting things to say. He has a sense of humor too. You never know."

CHAPTER 10

THE WEEK DRAGGED ON. SAMMY felt a void in his life, an empty space that could not be filled. He worked enthusiastically to distract from the ache in his heart, but he was only moderately successful. When he found himself with free time, he daydreamed about the beach in Gaza where he used to lie for hours hoping for better days.

His desk phone rang. Heart suddenly in his throat, Sammy considered whether he should answer it, knowing there was a good chance it was John. With a tense sigh, he picked up the receiver.

He was thrilled to hear John's voice but worked to keep his responses even. He didn't want to show his excitement. The conversation was brief. John was just checking in on him and his work day. Sammy purposefully cut the call short, not wanting to extend superficial pleasantries. He promised to call John back later that day. But he never did.

Friday came.

Despite his desire to make a clean cut, Sammy felt he owed John at least one last phone call. Reluctantly, he called. It shamed him how pleased John sounded to hear from him. "What are you doing tonight?" asked John. "Do you have any plans? I'd like to see you."

"Sorry, not tonight. I want to write to my mother tonight. I haven't written to her in a long time. And I need to pay bills. Do some things around the house." Sammy knew the excuses were lame but could think of no others.

"I miss you, Sammy," John murmured. "I want to see you."

John sounded pained, which upset Sammy greatly. He wanted to see John too. But he didn't want to sound desperate or otherwise hurting. "Yeah, fine. We can meet tonight," he stubbornly agreed. He couldn't help the stupid smile pulling at his lips. "The coffee shop?"

"Yeah." John's happiness was contagious. "How about around 8:00?"

Sammy got ready that evening, checking his reflection in the mirror countless times. He left the house early, eager to get there, and arrived around 7:30. John walked in some two minutes later.

"You're early," Sammy remarked.

"You are too," replied John, grinning.

"Well, that's good. I can only stay for an hour or so," continued Sammy, scanning the overhead menu.

"Well, would you mind if we got something to eat instead then?" John appeared startlingly handsome in his casuals. "I didn't eat lunch. We could go next door to the Chinese restaurant. The food's decent, and they're fast."

Seeing no harm in it, Sammy agreed.

They sat at a small table, exchanging few words. They made small talk about their jobs and other shallow things. Sammy remained tense. He could tell John wanted to talk about serious issues but was purposefully holding back. Eventually, it came to a head.

"Sammy… I want you to understand that I don't hate you. I have never hated you. It's the opposite. I like you very much. It's just… my father. He's concerned. You know how fathers are. He's never met you. He's just holding onto his old views, and I know that he's wrong. He doesn't know you, so he can hate you from a distance. Honestly, I don't understand it. Since I met you, I've read much about the conflict. And I think I have a better understanding of everything. I don't think my father's opinion really affects me."

Sammy kept his tone even. "But he *has* affected you. You came to me with questions and-and suspicions. And it hurt." He sighed. "Maybe we shouldn't talk about this."

A few moments of silence filled the air with rising tension. Sammy met John's gaze. He could see in John's eyes that he was hurting, just like Sammy. There was much they wanted to say but they kept it under the surface, struggling to rationalize it all.

John eventually opened his fortune cookie and read aloud, "Children should not pay the price for their parents' mistakes."

That seemed too on-the-nose for it to be a real fortune, and Sammy sighed, his eyes moist. "I agree." He was charged with emotion. He wanted to tell John how much he missed him, how much he loved him. He wanted all of this to stop, for everything to go back to the way it was. Instead, he looked the other way to hide his emotions.

But John noticed. He took Sammy's hand. "I will *never* hurt you again. I promise."

"I think… I need some time to myself. I'm sorry."

John didn't let go. "What are you doing Sunday? Maybe we could spend more time together then. Do brunch maybe? Or even a walk in the park?"

Sammy withdrew his hand. "I'll call and let you know. I'm not sure right now."

He returned home a little past 10:00 and wandered up to his room. He peered out the open window into the dark, as if trying to discern something from the great dim. But what needed elucidation was the maelstrom of emotions that swirled within him. Hoping that writing to his mother would ease his spirit, Sammy sat at his desk.

After struggling to begin, he considered just writing to her as an escape and not ever sending the letters. He could share with her about the real him, about John, about life in America—and never send them. So, that's what he did.

Dear Mother,

I need your advice. This is the time when I need you the most. I don't know what to do. I am in love, Mother. With a man. A man who I'm not supposed to be in love with. He's supposed to be my enemy. Or the son of my enemy, as I was taught.

But he's a good man, Mother. If you met him, you'd never hate him. I know you would still tell me no, that I shouldn't continue with him. But don't worry—I came to that conclusion myself. But maybe it's time for old animosities and hatred to disappear.

I am sick and tired of it all, aren't you? You must be. It wasn't easy for you, I remember, when my brother was killed. It wasn't easy for me or for the family. The neighborhood was devastated by it. But we had to move on. Our lives kept going. We must live and make the best out of what we have. Maybe we can stop hating if we try. Maybe we can replace hatred with love.

As for me, Mother, I have never hated John. I don't know how, but I just started loving him one day. I didn't know he was Jewish until later. I had no chance to hate him. I loved him first; it was the same for him. He did not know when we met that I was Palestinian. He had no chance to hate me. He loved me.

Unfortunately, we realized that love's not enough though. That other things—like where we come from, our religion, our heritage—are just as important. But I tell you the truth, Mother. Our differences never interfered with us loving one another.

Maybe I am wrong. Maybe you are right. In John's case, his father is telling him to hate me. His father hates me without seeing me.

Mother, I need your advice. Please write.
Your son,

Sammy

Sammy stared down at the letter for a long moment and then sighed. He needed something he could actually send.

Dear Mother,

I am always thinking of you. I miss you very much.
I'm doing well in America. My job is good and my health is well. I'm planning to come visit you next year on my vacation.

Write to me. Tell me about the whole family. And say hello to everyone for me. I miss them all. I'm sending you some money. I understand that Father does not make enough anymore. Perhaps this will help!

I love you.
Your son,

Sammy

He reread what he had written, conscious that the way he reacted to the world around him was still very Middle Eastern, very Palestinian. He needed to learn to better hide his emotions, especially when it came to John.

Sammy went downstairs in search of Michael, but upon finding him not home—which was odd—he returned to his room. Sometime later, the front door opened. Confused as to why Michael was returning home so late, Sammy ventured downstairs clad in nothing but his underwear to find Michael accompanied by a middle-aged man. Embarrassed, Sammy apologized and hurried back to his room to retrieve his robe.

"Sammy," greeted Michael with a smile, "this is Patrick. I've known Patrick for a long time, but I haven't seen him in several years. He's visiting from Milwaukee. I ran into him at the bar. I told him he could stay over with us. He's leaving tomorrow morning."

Sammy greeted him, trying to recover from the abrupt intrusion. Patrick was in his mid-fifties and boasted a medium build and pale complexion. His green eyes were startling and contrasted with his gray-brown hair. He had a warm, inviting smile.

"Oh, Patrick and I lost touch there for a while. It was a pleasant coincidence that we ran into each other tonight. I'm so happy to see him. He used to visit when Joseph was still alive. At the time, we lived on the north side of Chicago. Those were the good old days, don't you think, Patrick?"

Patrick sighed wistfully. "Yes, very nice. No fear of AIDs, and people were different, much friendlier, I would say. Those were indeed the good old days."

Conversation eventually turned to work, and Sammy learned that Patrick owned a gay bar in Milwaukee. It was a dance club but not as big as the ones in Chicago.

"I like dance clubs," Sammy remarked.

"You should come visit me in Milwaukee and come to my club," Patrick replied.

"So? How was your day?" asked Michael of Sammy.

"Eh, it was fine. I wanted to talk with you, but it can wait until tomorrow. Nothing urgent." Sammy excused himself to his bedroom as Patrick and Michael continued to talk, reminiscing.

After struggling to sleep for what seemed like an eternity, Sammy rolled toward the open door. He heard Michael and Patrick coming up the stairs. He watched from his darkened room as they entered Michael's bedroom.

Confused, Sammy almost thought to go help get the guest bedroom in a better state, but then it dawned on him that perhaps Patrick was staying over not just as a simple guest. He waited for Patrick to leave Michael's bedroom, for them to finish talking, but he never did.

CHAPTER 11

SATURDAY MORNING WAS A PLEASANT affair. Sammy made coffee and sat on the back patio as usual. He turned on the bird fountain and admired the flowers as he scanned the newspaper.

As always, he remained attentive to Middle Eastern news, going straight to the international section of the paper with the hope that something good had happened. When all he found were more stories of bombings, killings, and death, he contemplated whether he should even keep up hope. Frustrated, he tossed the newspaper to the ground and angrily sipped his coffee. He chatted with God briefly about the topic but was interrupted as Michael and Patrick joined him.

"Good morning," greeted Michael. "Talking to yourself this morning?" His roommate grinned teasingly.

"No, talking to God."

Michael's face fell.

Sammy motioned to the paper. "I keep wondering when all the war and violence is going to end. I just get so mad every time I read the newspaper. I talk to God because hopefully, one day, He'll listen."

"That's a bold request," Patrick replied solemnly.

"I just made coffee. Would you like some?" asked Sammy.

"Yes, please."

Once the conversation turned away from the news, the morning once again became enjoyable. They watched birds and talked about the garden, squirrels, and the weather.

Eventually, Patrick had to leave as Saturday nights were his busiest nights and he needed to head back home. Once he was gone, Michael and Sammy started Saturday morning chores. When they found themselves alone in the garden, Sammy decided to bring up what was bothering him. "Can we talk about John?" he asked. "I need your advice."

"Sure."

"I… don't know what to do with him. We talked for a while, and John held my hand and promised to never hurt me again. I think…" Sammy glanced at him. "I'm in love, Michael. What can I do?"

Michael's response was slow. "I know you're in love. Slow down. Good things will come your way; be patient and don't rush. Your relationship with John will fall in line."

"Sometimes I hate myself for loving him. I shouldn't love him like I do. We haven't been together for that long. But I can't explain it." He touched a nearby rosebud. "The roses are beautiful this year. Look at the unusual color on this one. It's almost purple." Remembering Joseph and then Patrick, he asked, "How long have you known Patrick?"

Michael continued to work, a smile on his face. "A long time. He's an old friend. When Joseph and I moved to Gaza for work, we lost touch. When we came back, we were all very busy, and then Joseph got sick."

"Patrick is a good-looking guy," Sammy said.

Michael said, "He takes good care of himself."

There was a short stretch of silence between them before Sammy asked, "I saw Patrick go into your room."

Michael chuckled. "We talked for a while. And yeah, we slept in the same bed. I had a crush on him for a long time when Joseph and I were together. I couldn't do anything about it at the time because I was with Joseph. But now he's here, and I found out that he had a crush on me. So… it happened."

Sammy smiled. "That's nice to fulfill a desire after so many years."

After lunch, Sammy tried to take a short nap as he hadn't slept well the previous night. But he couldn't sleep. Michael also lay down for a nap.

Sometimes Sammy felt inclined to drop everything and go somewhere where nobody knew him. His feelings were too intense, too strong. He didn't know how to handle them.

John was becoming a fixation, something Sammy thought about constantly. And in that regard, it was torturous. Sammy knew he needed to gain control of his feelings. He needed to identify them, give them names, and deal with them head-on. But that seemed like such a monumental task.

Later that afternoon when the phone rang, Sammy knew who it was.

"You getting ready for the party?" asked John.

"Yes, I am."

"So, are we still on for brunch tomorrow morning? We can take a walk through the park too. The weather is supposed to be nice."

"Yeah, is 11:00 okay? Same coffee shop on Halstead?" Sammy chided himself. He didn't want to seem too desperate or let his emotions control his every action. An internal dialogue of deprecation looped in his head.

The trip to the restaurant that evening was a short one. Michael gave directions from the passenger's seat as Sammy weaved through the Chicago streets.

"I talked to John," Sammy eventually said. "We're meeting tomorrow morning. I know... it's not right. But I can't help it."

Michael scoffed. "Why isn't it right? You enjoy seeing him. You'll have a good time."

Sammy shrugged as they fell into their respective thoughts. He didn't want to let his heart lead him. He was concerned and afraid that if he followed his feelings, he would experience more pain and disappointment. Perhaps he should try his hand at being calculating, cunning. Maybe *he* had to be the one to start doing the controlling and manipulating, but that was not in his nature.

The restaurant was in a country club on the outskirts of the city. It was lined with beautiful landscaping, manicured lawns, and tall evergreens. Carefully tended-to flowers adorned every flowerbed. They parked next to a car with four people—two men and two women—who had also just arrived, so they waited for the other guests to get out.

"We're going to be a few minutes early," said Sammy. "But I like that."

"Me too."

"Oh," said one of the other guests who must have overheard their conversation, "are you going to Jim's party?"

"We are," replied Michael.

"Are you a friend of Jim or new members of the club?"

"No, no, we're Jim's friends."

"Nice, very nice. My name is Ray."

"I'm Sammy."

They shook hands, and Ray introduced them to the rest of the group. "This is Jenny, Kris, and Tony."

As they started for the restaurant, Sammy leaned into Michael. "We're overdressed."

Ray and his group of guests were all in their late-forties and seemed to know where they were going as they found the room with ease.

"Oh good," whispered Michael. "Jim's already here."

Jim greeted all of them and ran through introductions quickly.

"Sammy, how is John doing? I should have invited him as well but didn't think of it."

"He's well," replied Sammy. "I just spoke with him before we left."

Distracted by arriving guests, Jim offered, "Help yourself to the bar. I hope you're both going to have a good time tonight."

Though Sammy doubted he would, he smiled nonetheless.

Guests trickled in until the restaurant's event room was full. Sammy noticed more men than women were present. Most looked relaxed as they joked and talked. They even hugged and embraced each other openly, which surprised Sammy. He exchanged furtive glances with Michael.

A short time later, Jim circled back around and introduced Sammy to new guests.

"Jim, you should have told me you knew such a nice-looking guy. You know I'm single," the guest teased.

Sammy was shocked.

"No, no," Jim laughed. "I think he's taken."

The guest met Sammy's gaze. "Are you taken, Sammy?"

A smile pulling at his lips, Sammy looked at Michael. "Yes, I think so. Maybe... It's complicated."

"Oh, is John just a friend?" interjected Jim.

Sammy lowered his voice. "No, we're, uh, dating… Jim, I thought we were coming to a straight party… How were you able to tell we're gay?" He motioned between himself and Michael. "We do a pretty good job acting straight, don't we?"

Jim laughed. "I don't know. I think I have some sort of radar, a sixth sense. I can feel it."

"Well, we didn't get that from you," Michael said.

"We never suspected you were gay," added Sammy, scanning the room. What he saw was a diverse group, a reflection of the gay community. It was a mixture of men and women who exhibited a wide range of masculine and feminine energy. He could easily discern some of the guests' proclivities, but others, he couldn't determine.

"I will tell you exactly how I found out," Jim explained proudly. "When I picked up John, his car had a rainbow flag sticker. Besides, when we were together in your backyard, I could tell that there was something between you and John. You reacted to him quite differently; it was very obvious. Your feelings just came out. It was cute. When you saw him, your eyes sparkled. You were so happy to see him, so attentive to him. I can tell, Sammy, when two people are in love."

Burning with embarrassment from Jim's most astute analysis, Sammy glanced at Michael who was grinning from ear to ear.

"Let me introduce you to the rest of my friends. I think you will get along with them; they will most certainly get along with you two."

Sammy followed Michael, allowing his older roommate to take the lead. Though they met numerous people, none stuck out as much as Jenny and Kris and Norman and Neal.

Jenny and Kris were a couple, but Norman and Neal were not. Norman was single, and Neal was also single, as far as Sammy knew. Jenny and Kris's two daughters lived with them. They told Sammy that they were happy their daughters had finished high school and were preparing to enter college. Norman was an attorney who was very proud of his sailing abilities and his sailboats and often spoke about his trips to Michigan. Neal was a wealthy businessman.

Enthralled by the array of different lives around him, Sammy thoroughly enjoyed himself and the conversation. The most interesting surprise was the entertainer named Ted, who was a member of the club. He was a playwright nearing eighty who used to be a teacher. He was vibrant and articulate and knew just how to get the crowd involved. He performed shortened plays and solos. Sammy found him inspirational and enjoyed watching him play different roles. He went to speak with Ted afterward and learned that the older gentleman had published plays. Ted's lover of forty years had passed and he was alone now, but Ted seemed happy.

Michael and Sammy were invited to become members of the club since the organization was by invitation only. They agreed they needed to take some time to think about it.

"Jim," cawed Michael, "this was such a wonderful get-together. It exceeded our expectations. You have a nice group of friends. Thank you so much for inviting us."

"This is my family," Jim explained. "The family I choose."

Michael and Sammy excused themselves. Michael drove since Sammy drank. On the way home, they recapped all that that they had seen and heard.

"Actually, I knew somebody there, someone I've known for several years. He used to date Joseph. They were together for a few months before he and I got together. We ran into him a handful of times; I know he never liked me. He thought I was the one who took Joseph away from him." Michael sighed. "He and Joseph broke up on bad terms."

"Who was it? Did I meet him?"

"Yeah, it was Neal."

"Oh."

"But we had a nice conversation. Neither of us has bad feelings anymore. We were both very cordial."

The discussion fizzled out after that as Sammy fell into thoughts about John and their impending brunch date. He was… looking forward to it.

CHAPTER 12

Sammy woke with a hangover. Peering into the mirror, he noted his pale complexion, swollen face, and droopy eyes. He considered how he was going to hide his condition from John. Perhaps he would feel better by their meet-up time.

With less energy than usual, Sammy made a large pot of coffee, as was Sunday morning tradition, and shuffled out onto the back patio to enjoy the fresh air, birds, and flowers. The sky was a deep azure that seemed to emphasize the fine weather and brilliant sun. After two cups of coffee and a large glass of water, Sammy moved on to trying a hangover remedy he had once heard about—tomato juice with raw eggs. Afterward, he took two aspirin, got dressed, and left to see John.

John was waiting for Sammy at the coffee shop. He greeted him warmly. Sammy had missed John; and the opposite was obviously true as John beamed at him. After some small talk, they decided on a restaurant with an outdoor patio where they requested a table in the sun. Multicolored flowers draped out of hanging pots around them and a small, nearby fountain trickled water, a lovely sound. Fresh flowers in clear vases brightened each table. The restaurant, which was a buffet-style eatery, was busier than expected. Sammy did his best to nibble on bland items.

Sammy described the party and its guests in detail, to which John lamented not being able to attend. It wasn't long before they fell into familiar conversation, having almost forgotten that they had been quarreling. How they moved around one another, their nonverbal communication, shifted and flowed naturally until it seemed as though they were talking without words. Glancing into John's gaze, Sammy thought, *I adore him so much. I love him.*

After filling his plate several times, John sat back away and groaned. "Oh, I ate too much. I probably just gained two pounds." He glanced at Sammy's plate. "You didn't eat." He scoffed. "And you look rough."

"I'm hungover…" Sammy admitted.

After their brunch, they left for the nearby park where they could meander about in the sunshine. The park, which was beautifully constructed and landscaped, gave way to a large manmade pond that boasted nearby trails. Walking those paths, they talked about life, what kind of relationship they each wanted to pursue, and if they wanted to see each other again—which they both did.

They eventually walked to Belmont Rocks, a poorly kept area of the park where gay men usually hung out to overlook Lake Michigan.

"This reminds me of home," Sammy murmured. "Of Gaza. We don't have rocks like these, but the water and the blue sky… and the warmth of the sun. All of it reminds me of home." He drew a long breath. "I'm thinking of going to see my family next year. I miss everyone, especially my mother."

"You should definitely go," John replied. "I can tell you're homesick." John reclined on his hands and peered out at the water. "What was it like coming to America for the first time?"

"A big adjustment. But Joseph and Michael prepared me. They had told me what to expect. Being around them, I learned a lot. But it was still a shock. It took a few years to adjust. Actually, I'm not sure if I'm fully adjusted even now."

John chuckled pleasantly.

"Did you know that I was fourteen when I first met Michael and Joseph?"

"I knew you've known Michael for a long time," John replied.

"Joseph spoke Arabic and taught English. When I first came here, I spoke very little English. Joseph and Michael lived in Gaza for a few years, a block from our house. We thought they were part of the U.N. or something, but I didn't know or care. They rented the second floor of a house, the prettiest house in the neighborhood. That's because it belonged to the wealthiest fisherman in the village.

He would always rent the second floor to foreigners who worked with human rights organizations or the United Nations. So, to us, Michael and Joseph were just more foreigners.

"I usually asked the foreigners if they had any need for extra help. You know, buying groceries, cleaning up, whatever. Just to make some extra money. So, when Michael and Joseph moved in, I asked if they needed help. They invited me in, and then Joseph immediately asked me if I had another pair of shoes." Sammy grinned sadly. "My shoes were literally falling apart. When I told them I didn't, Michael got me a pair of his shoes and had me try them on. They were a little big, but they were better than what I was wearing.

"They hired me to bring vegetables and fish from the markets." Sammy sighed. "I was the happiest boy. I had decent shoes and a job. I told them not to worry about the fish, that I would bring them all the fish they needed anytime.

"I started working early the next morning because I wanted to buy myself a new football and new clothes. I wasn't... the brightest kid in school, but I managed decent grades. My mother was proud of me even though I wasn't like my brother, Muhammad. He was so smart. The one who, uh, was killed. He always received high grades.

"But I didn't realize that Michael and Joseph didn't wake up so early. They let me in and told me how to make coffee and set the table. I was surprised because the apartment had been transformed. I had been there with other tenants and seen what they had done. But Michael and Joseph had made it look different, like a home. Framed pictures were on the walls; a painting with trees and angels that Joseph had painted hung above his bed. It caught me off-guard.

"I did their grocery shopping and brought them fish. They treated me so well. That summer was beautiful to me. I didn't want school to start up again in the fall."

"Tell me about school," interrupted John, interested.

"Well, it was limited. Very small. Everything was stripped down. The classrooms had benches and blackboards. That's it. The building itself was falling apart. It had a tin roof and tin doors; the windows had no glass," Sammy explained.

"Geez," John murmured.

"We'd sit two or three on a bench. We always ran out of chalk and had no books. The teacher would dictate, and we'd copy what he read. We had to hand copy materials from a few books that circulated."

"How long was school?"

"From seven until noon. We couldn't go in the afternoon because the building was used for other things. But that was okay. It gave me time to work at Joseph and Michael's house." Sammy smiled. "Eventually, I had saved enough money to buy new clothes, my new football, and new shoes. I was so proud…" Knowing what came next, Sammy continued more solemnly. "And then my brother was killed. I didn't go to school that day or to Michael and Joseph's. They knew about his death and came to offer their sympathies. But they didn't know how bad it was.

"A week or so passed. I didn't go to school or work. I just sat in my room, doing nothing. I didn't eat. I didn't go outside. I was no longer an innocent boy. I felt deep sadness and-and… anger. I cried and cried." Sammy struggled to pull himself from the memory. "Joseph visited, because he could speak Arabic, and talked to me about going back to work and school. I told him that I was afraid to leave the house, to even go outside. I was afraid to be killed. He couldn't… convince me otherwise."

Sammy fidgeted uncomfortably. "They visited me often and brought candy and chocolates, but I turned to skin and bones. I lost so much weight. One day, while I was sitting in the courtyard, I looked up to see birds migrating. As I watched, a single bird dropped right next to me, fluttering around. I picked him up and tried to get him back into the air, but he just couldn't do it. That day, I went outside our home for the first time in weeks, hoping that if the bird could see the others flying, it would join them. I hurried to the beach and I sat with him, watching.

"He never flew. Eventually, I took him back home. The next day, I brought him back to the beach and sat with him for hours, waiting for him to feel ready to get back into the sky. And he did. My heart filled with joy; I was so happy. The next day I returned to school and work. Joseph and Michael were so excited and surprised to see me that they didn't ask me to do anything that day. We just talked about school, my family, and how I was. I told them that I didn't think I would be able to keep working the same number of hours for them because I was so behind on schoolwork. Michael told me not to worry—and they kept paying me the same amount." Sammy looked out at the lake. "Look at the sky, the water… It's so beautiful."

"Yeah, it is," replied John.

"You know what?" Sammy stood. "I think I'm going to jump in." He jerked his shirt off and began unbuckling his pants. "In my underwear."

Grinning, John also stood. "I'm right there with you."

After stripping out of everything down to his underwear, Sammy leaped into the water. John joined him, splashing and whooping and hollering. Though the water was a bit chilly, mixed with the sun and warm air, it was refreshing. A few minutes passed before they clambered back onto the rocks.

Sammy shivered, despite the sun.

"Here, sit close. It'll help," said John. Sammy leaned into him so their shoulders touched.

As they shivered into each other and let the sun's rays dissipate the cold, they watched a sailboat slowly approach the area. When it anchored close to them, Sammy exchanged looks with John. It took him a minute to recognize one of the men waving at him from the boat.

"Oh!" exclaimed Sammy, standing. "It's Norman. I met him at Jim's party. He mentioned that he owns a sailboat."

"Ahoy!" shouted Norman gleefully. "Come on aboard!"

Sammy urged John to his feet, and together they leaped back into the water. "About to meet your new friend… in our underwear. How embarrassing," admitted John as they swam.

They climbed the sailboat's stern ladder and, shivering, Sammy introduced John to Norman. Norman greeted them and presented his friend Jeffrey who politely ignored the state of their attire.

"I know you…" Sammy murmured.

"And I know you… Do you work with Gaven's CPA?" asked Jeffrey.

"Ah! Yes, I do. I remember where we met. You work in the same building. You're a paralegal, right?"

"I am."

"I remember now. You came to our office. I talked with you for a short while." As Sammy finished explaining, he grew uncomfortable. Somebody who worked in the same building as him now knew about him… How could he stay hidden now? He hadn't come out yet; he wasn't *ready* to come out yet.

His thoughts turned angry and bitter as he chided himself for deciding to do something so dumb as to swim in his underwear.

While John continued to chat like the extrovert that he was, Sammy grew silent and withdrew. Whether John noticed or not, Sammy wasn't sure, but eventually, John suggested that they head back.

"I don't think I should go anywhere anymore," Sammy said once they were somewhat dry and dressed on the rocks.

"What? Why?" asked John, more amused than concerned.

"Because anywhere I go, I might meet someone who knows me. I'm afraid that guy might out me at work."

"And staying at home will solve the problem? What are you concerned about? Even if he outs you at work, nothing is going to happen."

"You don't understand," Sammy replied. "I have a very conservative boss. He might fire me. I know it's illegal, but he can do it. How can you prove discrimination? It's almost impossible. He'll find any excuse to fire me. I just don't want to give him that opportunity."

Ruffling the water from his hair, John asked, "Well, how do you know he's going to fire you? Society's changing. Gays are becoming more accepted."

"You don't know him. He's homophobic, says things all the time. Makes remarks and jokes about faggots and homos. It's so uncomfortable to be around him. Luckily, I don't have to talk with him often, but still…"

"Don't dwell on it too much. Would you care for a glass of wine? We could head back to my place."

"Yeah, that sounds good."

The walk to John's apartment was a pleasant one, but Sammy remained standoffish as he continued to fret about being outed at work.

They enjoyed a glass of wine, which went fast, and talked about the park and the spontaneity of their swimming expedition. Eventually, John suggested they retire to the bedroom. Setting his wine glass on the nightstand, Sammy noted the flashing answering machine in the corner of the room. "You're popular. Looks like you have three messages."

John crossed the room. "Well, let's find out who called."

The first message played.

"John, it's Dad. Hey, I just wanted to say that I'm concerned about you. Are you still hanging around that Palestinian guy? I thought we talked about distancing yourself from him. I don't get it, John. These people are terrorists. Please be so, so careful when you are with him. Don't bring him back to your apartment, don't be showing him—"

John pulled the answering machine cord from the wall, his face pale, and stared at the floor. "I'm… so sorry that…" He looked back at Sammy who stood on the other side of the bed. "He doesn't know what he's talking about. He's a prejudiced man, full of hatred. I'm… not like that."

Sammy numbly nodded and shuffled from the bedroom, overcome with shock and hurt. His fingers trembled, and his eyes filled with tears.

"Sammy, Sammy." John hurried after him. "Please, please." He took Sammy's hand, but Sammy refused to face him, to show him his tears. "Sammy, come on. Let's talk."

Gathering what calm he had, Sammy shook his head and withdrew. "No, I should head home. I need to… be by myself for a while. I'll get over it. I just need," he took a deep breath, "some time." John didn't try to stop him further.

When Sammy got home, he found the house empty. He went to his bedroom and began scanning an old album of Polaroid pictures, his eyes searching for the familiar and loving faces of his family.

By the time Michael came home, Sammy was in bed but not asleep. He heard him come in downstairs and then eventually make his way upstairs to his room. Sammy considered going to chat with him, but the phone rang, breaking the stillness of the house. Sammy glanced at the wall clock. It was 3:00 a.m.

He sat up as he heard Michael answer the phone and grew concerned when he recognized the stilted tones of Michael's shoddy Arabic. Stumbling across the hall, Sammy appeared in Michael's doorway. His roommate passed him the phone in the dim light, concern etched on his face.

The voice of Sammy's sister greeted him on the other end.

Sammy's father was gravely ill and was dying.

Sammy listened intently, his hand over his mouth as his sister hurriedly explained in the allotted time that if Sammy wanted to see their father before his passing, that he should hurry home.

Heart hammering, Sammy agreed to find a way home just as the operator interrupted them a third time and then disconnected the call.

"What's wrong?" Michael whispered.

"My father is really sick. They think he's dying." Sammy leaned in the doorway. "I have to go home in the morning."

"Okay, well, we'll look for airlines then and see what we can find," offered Michael, dragging him into his arms. "Oh, Sammy, I'm so sorry."

Sammy didn't sleep. Shortly after 5:00 a.m., he rose and began searching for airlines. When he found a flight to Israel for the following day, he purchased the ticket and then called John and explained all that had transpired. John came over that night.

They embraced in the foyer. "I'm so sorry. I hope you make it in time to see your father. I'm sure this is difficult for you. Is there anything I can do?"

Sammy shook his head.

"What time does your flight leave tomorrow? I can take you there."

"Five," Sammy grumbled. "That means I have to be there a little after three. You don't have to take me. I don't want you to get in trouble at work or anything."

"Nonsense, I'll do a half day and take you to the airport."

"How long are you planning to be gone?" asked Michael, joining them.

"Two weeks," replied Sammy. "That's all the vacation time I have. I was hoping to see everyone under… different circumstances, but that's not happening."

After a long embrace, John left. Sammy retired to his room to fill his suitcase, not paying attention to what he was taking or how he packed.

The following afternoon, John arrived around two to take Sammy to the airport. Once parked outside of departures, John helped Sammy unload his suitcase and stood beside his car. "I'm going to miss you, Sammy. You're an important part of my life now. I wish I could be with you at this difficult time."

"Yeah, me too," was all Sammy managed.

John withdrew a chain from his neck. The necklace had a gold seagull emblazoned on it. He slipped it over Sammy's head. "I can't go with you physically, but my spirit and thoughts will be with you. Touch the seagull every time you want to see or talk to me."

They embraced, and Sammy entered the airport. Preoccupied, Sammy didn't pay much attention to anything around him. How was he going to face it all? Would he even get to see his father alive again? In an emotional haze, Sammy navigated to his terminal, waited for his plane to arrive, boarded the metal bird, and took off for the other side of the world.

CHAPTER 13

THE PLANE LANDED IN TEL AVIV. Knowing he would have to take a taxi to Gaza, Sammy hurried through the gates. At the entrance of the terminal, a few people in civilian clothing stood observing the passengers. Sammy knew they were officials.

One of them pointed to Sammy and they drew him aside. More focused on getting back to Gaza in a timely manner to see his father rather than what awaited him, Sammy followed the officials to a separate room for interrogation. He was thoroughly searched and questioned about the purpose of his trip and what he had been doing in America. Sammy knew it was because he was Palestinian that he had been singled out. Others of Palestinian heritage had also been targeted.

Eventually, the officials, finding no reason to further keep him, released him, and Sammy sprinted from the airport. Of course, no one was there to receive him or was waiting for him outside. It would have been very difficult for anyone in his family to have done so as they had no car or money.

Finding a taxi proved just as difficult as he remembered as not many taxi drivers drove into the Gaza Strip. Finally, he hailed a taxi with a Gazan license plate and slid in with other passengers also en route to Gaza. He listened as the others spoke of their humiliating experiences at the airport.

The taxi was searched at a checkpoint, and Sammy was questioned again alongside the others he rode with. He felt like a stranger at home.

After entering Gaza, the scenery changed quickly. Rundown roads made for a bumpy ride. Demolished buildings and crumbling apartment complexes crowded every block. The stench of burning tires hung in the air. It felt like a war zone which, admittedly, it was. The Intifada, the Palestinian uprising that had begun in 1987, was winding down as negotiations between the Palestinian Liberation Organization and the Israeli government took place in Oslo, Norway. Though there was a cautious sense of optimism among the Palestinian people, it was tempered by the general state of their land.

Sammy's journey back into Gaza was an unpleasant one as he noted a lack of smiles on faces and the general despair that seemed to weigh on everyone's shoulders. After being gone for years, he had hoped to feel some excitement upon returning. But there was none. His heart hurt.

The taxi finally pulled into his neighborhood near the narrow alley down which his family lived. He thanked the driver and stepped out.

What awaited him at home? Was his father still alive?

Everything looked as though it were falling apart. A few kids played in the alley, and the door of the house was open like usual. As he approached, the children set off the alarm, shouting with delight. A familiar face appeared in the open doorway—Mariam, Sammy's youngest sister.

Mariam ran to him and hugged him hard, laying kisses on his cheeks as she cried. Sammy squeezed her tightly. After a moment, she quickly introduced the children who had greeted him. They were his nephews and nieces whom he had never met. After greeting them, he asked after his father.

"He's at the hospital," Mariam replied. "He's still alive, barely. Mother is with him now."

"I must go. Now," Sammy said, turning.

They flagged down another taxi along the main road. After a fifteen-minute drive down pothole-filled roads, they arrived at the hospital. It was crowded, rundown, and poorly equipped.

Sammy found his father in a mildly incoherent state. Though he recognized Sammy, he couldn't say much. Sammy held his hand and squeezed it tightly as his mother held onto Sammy and kissed him.

"It's been too long," she murmured into his shoulder. "I've missed you so much. We think of you all the time. Your father and I talk about you often. We always worry about you living in America. We hear life is difficult over there, that people don't care about each other. There is so much violence. I wish you would come back and live with us."

Sammy chose to ignore the statement. "How is he?" he asked, gesturing to his father. "What's happened? What has the doctor said?"

His mother pursed her lips. "There is no hope. It's cancer. It has spread all over his body. We did not know until it was too late. He had some difficulties and pain before, but we thought it would go away. We didn't think anything was wrong with him." She sighed. "And you know how much he hates to go to the doctor. They are too far away and too expensive. So, when the doctor found it, it was… too late. They told us he has only a few days to live."

Sammy looked away from his mother to hide his pain.

Zienab, one of Sammy's sisters, entered the hospital room. Sammy greeted her warmly, noting the traditional clothes she wore— a long dress that dusted the floor and was adorned with beautiful needlework along the neck, sleeves, and hem. Her hair was covered in a long, white cloth. She wore no makeup, but she didn't need it as she was naturally beautiful. Still, she appeared worn and unhappy. Sammy wondered if it was because of the circumstances or if she was generally unhappy with her lot in life.

He visited with his sister and mother for a long while, catching up on their lives, their families and health, and the local happenings. That evening, when he returned home, he was overwhelmed by the smell of fish. His heart sang.

Later, his brothers, sisters, nephews, and nieces filled the house. Some of the littles he knew, but others he had never met. He looked at every face, hugging and kissing each. Only his father and his brother—the bright one—were missing.

Naturally, all conversation was in Arabic. But occasionally, Sammy would slip in an "okay" or "yeah," and everyone would laugh.

"So, you became an American," his mother teased. "You forgot your Arabic."

Sometimes, he paused to recall an Arabic word, which was embarrassing, but the more he spoke, the easier it got. At times, conversation shifted back to their father in the hospital and the atmosphere grew sad. They talked about his difficult life as a refugee and losing not only his home in Jaffa but his son, Muhammad. Their father's craftsmanship, perseverance, and innovation when fixing fishing nets were unmatched, and the village considered him to be one of the best fishermen around. But above all, they shared stories of how he was a good father. He was a kind, loving, giving, and caring man.

Tears streaming down her face, Sammy's mother said, "We've been married for a long time. We've had both good and bad times. We've gone through everything together. He was always good to me." Everyone started crying.

As the evening wore on, many family members retired to their respective homes. Sammy noticed that his sister Fatima's husband hadn't shown up and so asked softly, "Where is he? Why isn't he here?"

"He's in jail. He's been in jail for a month," she replied.

"Why? Did he do something wrong?"

Fatima shook her head. "We don't know why he was detained. They call it administrative detention. He hasn't been charged yet. We don't know what he's being accused of, but there are indications they might release him soon. The soldiers came and searched the house so many times. They couldn't find anything. There's no evidence against him. I know he's not involved with anything." She was angry, frustrated. "I'm left with the kids, alone. If he doesn't work one day, we don't eat. I'm depending on my parents. They help us some, but it's been very hard on me. On the children. On his parents. His mother cries day and night. He is their only son."

Unsure of what to say to comfort his sister, Sammy offered, "I hope they'll release him soon." He felt helpless. There was nothing he could do to ease her pain or correct the situation.

"The Israeli soldiers," his sister continued, "they came into our house after midnight when we were sleeping. They knocked on the door violently and woke everyone up. The children were crying, frightened. When the door was opened, they rushed in and cuffed Hussein and took him away." She glanced at the children. "Now, every time they see an Israeli soldier, the children hide. They fear the soldiers will take them too."

Eventually, the house emptied until Sammy was left with just his mother and Mariam. He was tired. His mother fixed his bed like she had when he was growing up, and he lay down to ponder on the events of the day. His brother-in-law was in jail; his father was dying in a hospital; everyone appeared to be in terrible physical, mental, and emotional health. How were children fed and kept safe? How were children sent to school in such a violent and chaotic environment?

They went to the hospital the next morning. He was still alive but unconscious. Around noon, the rest of the family arrived and surrounded the patient's bed. Sammy's oldest brother suggested that they turn his father to face the *Qibla*, to face toward Mecca, the house of Abraham, for prayer. This would also grant their father easier access to heaven, so they moved him accordingly. As if he had been waiting for that moment, Sammy's father left them a few minutes later. The room filled with sobs and quiet cries.

It took but a few hours for his father's body to be transported to the family home. Everyone was there—brothers, sisters, aunts, uncles, nephews, nieces, and neighbors. They came to say their goodbyes.

According to Muslim tradition, the deceased needed to be washed; thus, the man whose job it was to wash the recently deceased arrived punctually and began the process. Sammy and his brothers helped. Afterward, they wrapped his father's body in a white cloth and placed it atop a wooden bench. They carried him to the mosque for the funeral and then to the cemetery. All men present helped carry the body, changing pallbearers while they proceeded as was tradition. The cemetery was about two miles from their home, so it took them quite a while to get there. Once they arrived, they buried the coffin and then went home.

People began arriving to pay their respects to the family. Per tradition, a recital of the Koran followed. The house was packed. Neighbors provided food for that night and the next few days.

Aside from wrestling with the general melancholy of the event, Sammy remained standoffish as he didn't know how to interact with the steady influx of guests. He felt out of place. The issues people discussed were obtuse to Sammy, so his replies felt insincere. Especially when they began talking about politics. It was something they couldn't avoid discussing; it was an intimate part of their lives. Still, Sammy tried to provide noncommittal remarks before allowing his mind to drift. He thought of his family, of the bright one, of the beach, of the birds and, at times, of John.

The following three days were spent receiving guests from morning until night. Men and women were separated with the men in the court of the house and the women in the receiving room, which was converted at night into a bedroom for the girls. After the three days, mourning ended, and the number of people visiting the house lessened substantially.

On the fourth day, Sammy decided to make a trip to the beach. He wanted to play in the sand and hug the water. He wanted to feel the warmth of the sun and to feel his childhood again.

So, he went to the same place he had visited as a child.

It was just a piece of beach, but he called it his own.

So many times, he had sat there and dreamed. He had slept there, played there. And he had built castles in the sand and air there.

He had dreamed of living in the same village as his family, having a small house with a wife and children. He had dreamed of owning a fishing boat and learning the craft of fixing nets from his father.

But none of those dreams had come true.

Sammy sat on his beach for almost two hours, dreaming and remembering. He smiled and cried as he reminisced and thought about the hardships of life. All his childhood dreams had evaporated.

From his spot on the beach, he could see the place where Michael and Joseph had once lived and where he had worked. They had changed his life. In fact, it had been Joseph who had asked him what he thought about college.

"I don't think I'm going," Sammy had told him. "We don't have money. My father cannot support me in college. So, it's impossible to go."

"What if you go to America?" Joseph had asked.

Sammy had opened his eyes wide. "America? No… It's impossible. I can't go there. If we sell all the fishing equipment and nets, maybe we can afford one ticket. But that's it. It is out of the question, Joseph."

With a twinkle in his eye, Joseph had replied, "Work hard. Let's see what we can do for scholarships."

One day some months later, he had surprised Sammy with a home visit, extending to him a piece of paper. "You're going to America. You've been granted a scholarship to study in America."

That scholarship had completely changed Sammy's life. Of course, the family's reaction had been mixed. His mother had opposed the idea as she couldn't imagine her baby going to America to live and learn in such a violent society. But his father had supported it. "Let him go," he had said. "He might have a better future there."

Sammy stayed on the beach until the sun set and then returned home. The house once again smelled nostalgically of fish. Mother was cooking sardines like usual. Although it was not sardine season, she had searched extensively for them. It was the most delicious meal Sammy had ever had.

"I must tell you something about Mariam," his mother said later that evening. "Somebody you know, an old friend of yours—Shaker—has asked for her hand in marriage. We told him we would think about it. Then your father got sick, and we couldn't decide then. I know he is waiting for a response. I am going to consult with your brothers and sisters to see what they have to say."

Shaker had been Sammy's classmate. They had played together often, perhaps a little *too* often. He couldn't tell his mother that the playful touching they had engaged in had led to other things. They hadn't had sex, but it was close enough.

"And... how does Mariam feel about this proposal?" asked Sammy, carefully turning the conversation.

"You can ask her yourself. Times have changed. She's the one who has to decide," his mother replied.

Sammy glanced at his sister who was washing dishes. "How do you feel about him?"

Mariam shrugged. "I don't feel anything for or against him. He is just another man."

"Would you marry him? Are you willing to spend the rest of your life with this guy?"

"I am not sure, but it's a possibility. He is not a bad-looking man, and he works."

Sammy did not know how to respond, what to say. He had forgotten that that was how life was in Gaza. But how would he face Shaker in the future with the memories of what they had done together?

Moments of silence passed. His mother asked what he was thinking, whether he approved.

Sammy tried to smile. "It's not for me to approve. It's for Mariam." He hoped his sister would decline the proposal or that one of his brothers would object. But none of them had.

The following day, Shaker came by. At the funeral, Sammy had met him formally, and they hadn't talked much. Now, it was different. They hugged and exchanged cheek kisses, as was customary, and Sammy pretended that he didn't remember anything. Though the matter was never brought up, he thought about it constantly.

Shaker asked about life in America and what Sammy did and how he spent his time. He asked questions about American women and how they treated him, solemnly advising him not to marry an American woman.

Eventually, Sammy's mother told Shaker to bring his family so that they may make the engagement official and read the *Al-Fatah*, a chapter of the Koran which begins the engagement period.

Three days later, the men of Shaker's family came over to meet the men of Mariam's family. When Shaker's father stood and asked for Mariam's hand in marriage for his son, Mariam's oldest brother approved. Then, all the men present read the *Fateha*. Mariam officially became engaged.

No celebration was allowed because her father had been deceased for only a few days and tradition specified that forty days had to pass before they could have any celebrations. Sammy thought it provided Mariam a good opportunity to consider her decision before it became irreversible.

With only a week left in Gaza, Sammy wanted to spend it walking through the neighborhoods or along the seashore, collecting shells and swimming. But he had forgotten how restricted his movement was as every time he tried to leave the house, his mother warned him to take care, that it wasn't safe out and that he might get caught in a confrontation between protesters and soldiers. Still, Sammy tried to make the most of his visit.

He found time to get back out to the beach and was able to visit his old high school and Joseph and Michael's old house. He went to a playground where he watched children play and was eventually invited to take part in the games. The kids joked and laughed with him as they knew he had been living abroad in America; they were curious. They asked many questions about life in America, to which he always responded, "It's wonderful and beautiful."

He made a trip to Gaza City via taxi, which he shared with others, and walked the main street to the center of the city. The air was tense, and the buildings were in disrepair. When an army jeep whirred by, everyone—including Sammy—became aware of what was about to happen and broke into a run in the opposite direction. Sammy followed others as seconds later, stones and gunfire were exchanged the next block over. While fourteen- and fifteen-year-olds, frustrated with the Israeli occupation of their land, threw rocks, soldiers fired haphazardly.

The following day, Sammy opted for the beach once more. He sat at the spot where he used to lounge and looked out at the waves. Few people were out. He enjoyed the sound of the water crashing on the white sand and the sunshine and solitude. His mind wandered until he found himself missing John.

It was then that he realized that not only did he miss John, but he missed... home? Wasn't he home? Wasn't Gaza home? Wasn't it where his family was, where his house and history were?

Sammy contemplated this as he felt his heart shudder in disagreement. He could no longer relate to people in his family, to the struggles of their daily lives. He missed Michael's enduring wisdom and level-headedness and John's unconditional love and openness. He missed the privacy of his room and the freedom to move about— the freedom to be himself.

Holding the seagull necklace, Sammy focused on this realization. He hadn't taken the necklace off since he had arrived and so clung to it as a symbol of his splitting identity.

With the sun high overhead, Sammy stood, dusted himself off, and went home. Lunch was ready when he arrived. He ate and then took a nap.

That afternoon, Sammy became the center of attention as his brothers and sisters discussed finding him a wife. One of his sisters-in-law recommended a girl in the neighborhood as a suitable match, and Sammy agreed that he would meet her if he had the time. His brother saw through his response though and urged him to go, telling him that he must get married as there was nothing more enjoyable than being married and settled with the right wife.

Sammy smiled politely, recognizing that his brother, Ahmad, had found marital bliss while his sister had not. His brother had discovered happiness in marriage; his sister had lost the spark in her eyes. When he was finally alone with Hend, his sister, he softly asked if she had ever considered divorce.

"How could you even ask such a thing?" Hend replied. "No way. I have children. They are the most important thing for me in my life. Besides, I can't get a divorce even if I want one. The man decides."

"Yes, I'm sorry. I forgot that. The men decide everything here," replied Sammy.

When among his family, Sammy felt at home, comfortable. Other times, he felt like a stranger in a strange land, unable to understand or relate. It irked him.

The call to prayer reverberating on the loudspeakers across the city woke him the next morning. He was tempted to go to the mosque but opted to stay in bed because he had not practiced Islam since he had left. After breakfast, he went directly to the beach, to the same spot, and lay down on the sand to watch the water and sky. He observed the birds soaring overhead and the deep, azure sky. It was another beautiful summer day. Time seemed to stop.

An hour or so later, he returned home to eat lunch and visit with his mother.

Feeling sentimental, he ventured to Michael and Joseph's old house, which now had new foreign tenants. Neighbors informed him that the new renters were from Sweden and worked for the United Nations.

The house had looked better when Michael and Joseph had lived there. It had been well-painted and boasted a beautiful garden. Studying the home now, he couldn't help but compare its drab appearance. Michael and Joseph had injected such amazing energy and love into it at the time. Looking back, Sammy could discern how it had been the place where he had learned that he had a tendency for men. Of course, neither Joseph nor Michael had ever flirted with him; in fact, they had tried to hide their homosexuality from him. But Sammy had found out anyway.

Fridays had been his off days from school, so he had spent that time working in Michael and Joseph's house. Normally, he arrived around nine, but one Friday, he had arrived unexpectedly at seven, thinking that he would do the garden work first and not wake them.

After climbing the stairs to the balcony that overlooked their bedroom to water the flowers up there, he heard them talking. Though the blinds of their window were down, there was a small hole in one of the slats. Glancing through it, he found them naked, holding each other tight. Startled, his heart beating wildly, he rushed back down the stairs as quickly and quietly as he could. He hadn't known what to make of it; he had never seen anything like it before… And he was tempted to go back and take another peek.

He had flirted and experimented with other boys, but Michael and Joseph were adult men. That realization weighed on him. Perhaps his fascination with the same sex *wasn't* just a phase.

Unable to continue working, he went to the beach to wait until his designated time of arrival.

At 9:00, he returned to their home to find them sitting on the porch, drinking coffee. Sammy tried to act normal, as if nothing had happened. He was a little afraid of them, that they would take advantage of him. For a few days, he distanced himself from the pair, pondering on and hating the fact that his homosexuality might be a lifelong struggle. But as the days went by and nothing happened, he grew more accepting of what he had witnessed and life went back to normal for him.

The last year of high school, however, changed that as he had found himself head-over-heels in love with a handsome boy named Hasan. Of course, Hasan had no interest in him as he was focused on girls. Seated in Michael and Joseph's yard, depressed indeed, Sammy had tried to wrap his head around the feelings that loomed so large in his heart. Joseph joined him.

"What's wrong? You look sad."

Sammy hadn't been able to stop himself. "Yes, I feel something about one of my classmates, and it's consuming me day and night. I think… I'm in love with him."

Joseph hadn't appeared surprised. On the contrary, he had seemed amused and understanding. "One day you will find the love of your life. Until then, be strong."

Eventually, the time came for Sammy to return home. He found Mariam alone, as their mother had gone to the market to purchase vegetables. She offered Sammy a cup of coffee, and he took the opportunity to sit with her and talk about her future husband.

"Do you like him?" he asked.

"I don't dislike him," she replied. "But I'm not in love with him." Quickly, she added, "Like they say, love comes after marriage."

Sammy considered telling her about his experiences with Shaker, but every time it was on the tip of his tongue, he fell silent and his heart raced. "Well, maybe you—"

Gunfire erupted outside, startling them both. Sammy leaped for the open door and peered outside. People were running in every direction. Where was their mother? Why wasn't she back already?

"Come on," Mariam said from across the room. "These things happen all the time. The children throw stones at the Israeli soldiers, and the soldiers shoot back."

Luckily, a few minutes later, their mother returned, and Sammy was relieved. She reported that the market had closed down. Shortly thereafter, curfew was announced on the loudspeakers.

"We just had a long curfew not long ago, right before you came home," his mother continued, seemingly unbothered. "It lasted for three days. I hope this one will be shorter. I have food at home but not enough to last that long."

"I… have to leave. I have to fly back to America in three days," Sammy replied.

His mother looked up to the sky and opened her hands and asked God for mercy on their family, for Him to remove the bad days and to rid them of the oppression of their occupier. "They think they are powerful, God," she said, "but You are the most powerful. We can't do anything about it, but You can."

God heard his mother.

The curfew lasted for twenty-four hours.

Sammy spent the time visiting with his family, discussing his sister's marriage, and discerning how his mother was going to live by herself. Upon speaking of their now-deceased father, his mother cried frequently. Her life was not going to be the same without him.

The following afternoon, once the curfew was lifted, Sammy's family, his new brother-in-law included, and neighbors gathered to bid him farewell. At times, he wanted to blurt out to Mariam all that had transpired between him and Shaker as he was concerned that she was marrying a homosexual man, but he held himself back. Maybe Shaker had changed. Maybe it had just been a passing, teenage fancy.

When conversation turned to Sammy and when he was going to marry, he grew uncomfortable. They lined up girls for him to choose from and even had women who, his sisters claimed, could live in America. "She just finished high school and can speak a little English," Hend said. "She is nineteen."

Sammy remained polite but standoffish, providing noncommittal responses and remarks. The more he looked at his brothers and sisters and their spouses, the more he knew that that lifestyle wasn't for him.

Had he never left Gaza, perhaps he could have repressed everything and married like a normal man. He'd have a wife and children by now, living a simple life. But moving to America had changed him. Sexual encounters hadn't cut it. He had discovered that he wanted to be in a relationship with someone, to share a life with someone.

With some clarity, Sammy realized that when he was in America, he looked forward to going home to Gaza. But now that he was in Gaza, he wanted to go back to America… to where home was. Although he still felt very Palestinian in America with his feelings, culture, traditions, and accent, his thinking had changed.

Was he a Palestinian in America?

Or was he an American in Gaza?

Sammy rose the following morning before the sun. A taxi was waiting for him. His mother and sister saw him off.

"Do not marry an American girl," his mother chided him. "We have good girls here for you. They will suit you better. They will be able to understand you. You know that Palestinian girls make good wives."

Although everything in him refused her words, he politely agreed. He hugged and kissed Mariam and then slid into the taxi. As the cab passed Michael and Joseph's old house, Sammy clung to the seagull necklace around his neck. He was leaving the place where it had all begun.

There were checkpoints where soldiers searched cars and travelers. After waiting in line for an hour, both Sammy, the driver, and the car were thoroughly searched. At the airport, they were searched again by more soldiers as cars from Gaza had a separate lane from the Israeli cars. Inside the airport, Sammy and his luggage were checked again, causing him to be the last one to board the plane. Only when the plane took off was Sammy able to relax.

The one thing he had taken from Gaza was a bit of sand and some shells from his spot on the beach. Once he landed in

Amsterdam for a two-hour layover, he picked up a box of cigars for Michael and a bottle of cologne for John. His flight to Chicago was an uneventful affair. Upon spotting a familiar scene—Lake Michigan and the spectacular skyline—Sammy grinned, his heart elated.

He was home again.

CHAPTER 14

Going through customs in Chicago, Sammy couldn't help but compare the cruelty and humiliation he had experienced in Tel Aviv to the American system. He felt as if he were being welcomed home. Luggage in hand, he strolled out among the crowds of people waiting to receive loved ones and was surprised to spot John.

John excitedly waved both hands upon seeing him, a large smile spread across his face. Sammy couldn't help the joy he felt and jogged to him. They embraced deeply and then kissed, oblivious to the people around them.

"Oh, I'm so glad you're back. I missed you," John hummed into his neck.

"I'm glad to be back. I missed you too. And I missed everything about America."

Once in the car, they shared another kiss before setting off out of the airport. Sammy tried to keep the conversation light and vague. He didn't want to go into too much detail regarding all that had transpired in Gaza because he didn't want to expose John to the cruel reality of life there. John asked cautious and mildly probing questions but seemed to sense Sammy's hesitancy. For the time being, they were just content to be back together.

In the driveway, Sammy pulled the house keys from his carry-on and looked at them admiringly. How could something as simple as a house key provide him with such peace of mind? "Home sweet home," he mumbled to himself.

John helped him carry in his luggage. Michael was at work so the house was empty. The moment the front door closed, John advanced on Sammy. In a tangle of limbs and clothes, they raced upstairs, passionately kissing.

Sammy insisted on showering since he had been in an airplane for hours to which John readily agreed. Once the water was hot, they stepped into the shower and continued where they had left off. His hands running the length of John's body, Sammy rediscovered his love, pausing momentarily only to breathe. There was no need for words as John's excitement to be reunited was just as evident. At that moment, Sammy realized that there was more to their relationship besides sex. They were more connected than ever; something deep-rooted held them together, bound them. That revelation was transformative.

Anxious to indulge after their extremely pleasant if not exhausting shower, Sammy selected a nice bottle of wine, and they sat on the back patio to share the drink. John began prying again, delicately asking questions about Sammy's trip.

"I'm sorry," he sighed. "I was so, so worried. We hear in the news all the time about clashes between Israeli soldiers and Palestinian protesters, you know, throwing rocks. About people being killed. I was so worried about you, Sammy."

Unwilling to shatter the joy of their reunion, Sammy chose his response carefully. "The situation is dire. It's absolutely miserable over there. All I can say is that I'm glad to be back." Though guilt gnawed at his gut for having left his family, friends, and neighbors behind, he knew now that he envisioned his future in America.

John hugged Sammy. "I'm sorry you went through all that."

Sammy buried his head in John's shoulder, taking comfort in the warmth of his body.

An hour later, Michael arrived home and warmly greeted Sammy. He gave his condolences for the death of his father and imparted a long, loving embrace. Michael had known Sammy's father and had even spoken to him many times to persuade him to allow Sammy to leave to study in America. Michael's genuine remarks about Sammy's father touched him.

Of course, Michael asked questions about the trip as well, but his questions were different from John's. He asked about the village, the house he and Joseph had lived in, and about the people he had known at the time. By the time he had relayed all the information, Sammy was beyond tired and he was already starting to feel the effects of jet lag. John excused himself and left as Sammy went to bed.

The following morning, Sammy awoke without the aid of an alarm, confused. Realizing it was nearly time to get ready for work anyway, he rose and prepared for the day. He arrived at the accounting firm shortly after 7:30. No one was there. Eager to get to work, he began organizing for the day. There were two things he needed to get done—catch up on work and talk with John.

He called John just before 8:00.

"Hey you, did you sleep?" John teased.

"Yes. I, uh, I actually was calling," said Sammy, "to tell you that I can't stop thinking about last night. I never knew…" He lowered his voice even though he was the only one in the office. "I never knew that sex could be that good."

John chuckled. "I feel the same way. The best sex I've ever had in my life. You took me to a place I've never been. When am I going to see you again?"

"Oh…" Sammy thought. "I need to catch up on work. Can I call you later? I'll know more later in the day."

"Sure, that's fine. I'll talk to you later."

Sammy's coworkers arrived an hour later. The office wasn't large with only twelve employees present. Occasionally, they went out for a drink after work on Fridays, but other than that, they focused primarily on their work. In such instances, Sammy rode with Sue, a beautiful blond in her mid-twenties who had worked at the office for about two years. Although he had gone out with her to clubs and parties a few times, he had never ventured to share much of his personal life with her. When she asked questions about him, he deflected and managed to skip around them.

Sammy was warmly welcomed back by his colleagues and Sue, who gave him a warm hug.

John called later that afternoon. "Dinner tonight?"

Gazing at the pile of folders and documents beside him, Sammy sighed. "No. I won't be leaving for another few hours. Can we do it this weekend? Give me some time to catch up on sleep too. We could spend all of Saturday together."

"Yeah, that's fine." John's disappointment was obvious but he remained pleasant. "I'll see you Saturday then."

A few minutes later, Sue stopped by Sammy's desk. "We're so glad you're back. I was worried about you. We heard about the violence there and saw it on the news."

"Yeah," Sammy replied. "I'm glad I'm back too. It was a very difficult trip for me."

"Uh, at any rate," Sue leaned against his desk, "a friend of mine is getting married, and I was invited but I don't want to go by myself. Would you be willing to be my date? The wedding is four weeks from now."

Not seeing a problem with the invitation, Sammy replied, "I don't think I have anything planned that far ahead, so I should be able to make it."

"Oh, great! My friend comes from a super wealthy family, and they're having an elaborate wedding reception for her at the Four Seasons Hotel. I'll give you all the details later." Sue flashed him a smile and then scurried off.

The rest of the week went by in a flurry. All Sammy did was sleep and work. He and John talked on the phone daily. Friday after work, Sue invited Sammy to go for a drink with her and, having concluded most of his work, he shrugged and agreed.

They went to a local bar close to their office which normally grew crowded, especially on Friday afternoons. Sipping on a beer, Sammy peered out at the throngs of people speaking loudly to hear each other over the multitude of televisions and laughter. When he realized Sue was watching him, he met her gaze.

"You're quite handsome," said Sue. "Your hazel eyes are beautiful."

Suddenly shy, Sammy said, "Uh, thank you."

Fidgeting with her mug, Sue continued. "What are you doing tonight, Sammy? If you're free, we could go to a club, go dancing. If that interests you…"

"I'm actually really tired and would prefer to go home and sleep. I'm still jet-lagged from the trip. It feels like it's getting worse each day," Sammy replied, trying to keep his voice even. "Maybe some other time?" He knew what she was doing and considered whether he should tell her that he was homosexual. He didn't want to hurt her feelings or disregard her advances but he didn't want to lead her on either.

He hurriedly finished his drink, thanked her for the invitation, and left, not caring that he had just made everything that much more awkward.

When he arrived home, he found Michael and Patrick sitting on the patio sipping wine. He hadn't expected to see Patrick again but he was pleased for Michael. He joined them and drank coffee for a little while until he realized he needed to call John to finalize their plans. After agreeing to meet him the following day at noon at their coffee shop, he went straight to bed.

The coffee shop on Halsted Street was busy. From there, Sammy and John decided to go to a Spanish tapas restaurant in Boystown. They sat at a corner table on the outdoor patio, ordered sangrias, and talked.

"Okay, please tell me about your trip," John said. "I want to know everything. I know it wasn't pleasant, but I want to know what happened."

"Does it have to be right now though?" countered Sammy. "It's such a pleasant day and my memories are not pleasant. I'd rather talk about you and me."

John sighed. "Fine… Whatever you say, we will talk about." He gestured to Sammy. "You're still wearing the seagull." Sammy started to take the necklace off to return to John. "No, no, no. It looks good on you. I want you to keep it. It's a gift."

Sammy grinned. "Thank you… That means a lot to me. I held the seagull and thought of you many times when I was in Gaza, especially when I was sitting on the beach by myself. Whenever I held it, I felt your presence."

"Maybe next time we can go together," John said. "I'd like to see your village, the place where you were born and raised."

Sammy grimaced and looked away. "I don't think that's possible with the current situation in Gaza. It's dangerous there." A thought occurred to him and he met John's gaze. "So, tell me, are you still receiving those phone calls from your father, the ones telling you not to talk with me or see me?"

John swallowed a mouthful of sangria and shook his head. "He doesn't call me about that anymore. We haven't talked in a while."

After finishing lunch, they walked through the park toward Belmont Rocks, holding hands and discussing light-hearted matters like movies, music, and the people around them.

When a bicyclist approached, they stepped aside to give the large man more room. "Diseased, motherfuckin' faggots," the cyclist spat as he sailed by them. "I hope you die. The world's better off without you." And he was gone.

Sammy and John stared after the man, stunned. They exchanged looks and then glanced about to see if anyone else had witnessed the verbal assault. There was no one.

"Don't pay attention to him," said John, encouraging Sammy to keep walking. "There are many like him, ignorant people."

Sammy followed John. "That was the… first time that's happened to me."

"Not the first time for me," John replied. "One time, I was walking down the street from my building and I was beaten by two men because they suspected I was gay."

"What?" asked Sammy, alarmed.

"Yeah, they just got out of their car and beat me up real good. I was bleeding; they almost killed me." John's face was morose. "I've heard of instances where gay men have been killed. Look, don't think too much on it. Just be yourself. You don't look gay anyhow. Honestly, I don't think I look gay either. We aren't feminine or flamboyant. Maybe it's because we're holding hands." He made a disgusted sound. "Yeah, just forget that man. He's crazy."

Once they made it to the rocks along the lake, they sat with other gay couples enjoying the view. When a sailboat anchored a short distance out once more, John asked, "Isn't that Norman?"

Sammy studied the boat. "Yes, it is. He can't see us though. Let's wave."

Norman spotted them and motioned them into the water.

"Well?" asked John.

Having thought that they might visit the rocks, Sammy had worn his swimsuit and revealed it to John. John grinned and flashed his swimsuit from under his clothes. They had separately had the same idea.

They visited with Norman for a long while, sitting in the sun to dry off.

"Next week is my turn to host the Imagine Club Party. Would you like to come?"

John looked at Sammy. "I'm available. Do you have anything planned for next weekend?"

"No, nothing." To Norman, Sammy asked, "Could we have your phone number?"

Eventually, Sammy and John swam back to the rocks and sat there for a while longer before dressing. During their journey back through the park, Sammy self-consciously kept space between himself and John so as not to give the impression to anyone that they were together. He was so nervous and uncomfortable that John had to slow his pace.

"Sorry, I'm just hot," Sammy lied. "Do you want to go have a cold drink at the coffee shop?" Once he had his hands wrapped around a signature drink, Sammy remained aloof and preoccupied.

"What's wrong, Sammy?" John asked, mildly amused. "You're not communicating."

Realizing he was right, Sammy said, "I can't stop thinking about that man in the park. He made me feel awful."

"Eh, forget about it." John leaned back in his chair. "Look, what would you like to do tonight? We could do something fun, interesting. We could go see a movie or go out to dance. What do you want to do?"

"Honestly, I don't feel like doing anything." Sammy grinned slightly. "I just feel like sitting at home doing nothing. I'm sorry."

"Don't apologize. A lazy afternoon sounds good."

They looked into the windows of antiques stores for a while before heading back home. Michael and Patrick had already left. Sammy declared that he needed a nap, to which John agreed. While retrieving a glass of water to take upstairs with him, he noticed a note on the refrigerator.

I'm going to Milwaukee and will be spending the night there. I'll see you tomorrow.

–Michael

"Milwaukee, huh?" asked John, reading the note over Sammy's shoulder. "What's in Milwaukee?"

"Michael knows someone there. Patrick. I think they're… getting involved." Sammy shrugged. "Good for them. Let's go take a nap."

In the kitchen, John pushed Sammy against the refrigerator and kissed him teasingly. When Sammy couldn't take it anymore, he led John upstairs to his bedroom.

That evening, they cooked a quiet dinner and sat on the patio. Most of the time, they didn't say anything. They just touched, listened to music, and enjoyed the pleasant breeze. When Sammy asked John to stay the night, John readily accepted the invitation.

CHAPTER 15

Dᴜʀɪɴɢ ᴛʜᴇ ᴡᴇᴇᴋ, Sᴀᴍᴍʏ ɢᴏᴛ in touch with Norman to learn about the party's details. Saturday, Sammy and John met at John's apartment and went to Norman's. They arrived half an hour late to find the house already filled with people. Some faces were familiar, but many were not. Of course, Jim was there.

Norman greeted them at the door and then immediately got busy visiting with other new arrivals. Sammy and John gathered around Jim who was chatting with a young man in his mid-twenties.

"Ah, Sammy! John! I'm so glad you could come!" Jim beamed. "This is C.J."

C.J. was alarmingly handsome and boasted a crown of thick, black hair.

"C.J., what do you do for a living?" asked John, politely starting conversation.

C.J. grinned. "I'm a dancer. I dance at gay clubs, and I'm a model. I don't have a big job modeling but I'm working on that." When he shared with them the name of the club that he worked at, John and Sammy exchanged furtive glances. That club was known for having male hustlers. After a few more minutes of conversation with C.J., they determined that he was a male escort.

Only once introductions pulled them away from Jim and C.J. did Sammy come to realize that C.J. was the party's entertainer as he gave a provocative strip show to the crowd's delight. Sammy found it amusing.

Norman's house was enormous and beautifully decorated with expensive furniture. It had a vast back porch that overlooked a pristine swimming pool, and every window of the house was decorated with a menagerie of plants as if it were a tropical garden. Norman had hired a bartender and a waiter and provided catered food with different meats and salads. The bar was fully stocked with all kinds of liquor and drinks, including Sammy's favorite, twelve-year-old Dewar's, which he drank all night.

The party teemed with laughter and lightheartedness. Everyone was having fun.

To Sammy's chagrin, he once again met Norman's friend, Jeffrey, who worked in the same building as Sammy. He remained pleasant and polite but wondered if he should tell him not to say anything to his coworkers. In the end, Sammy decided to stay quiet and hope Jeffrey knew to keep the events of the weekend a secret.

As the evening wore on, partygoers took to leaping into the pool. Though Sammy felt drawn to swim as well, he didn't have a swimsuit, and he wasn't about to strip down.

"There's plenty of food and drinks!" Norman called. "Please enjoy yourselves." To John and Sammy, he said, "I'm so glad you came."

"We're having a great time," replied John. "You have a beautiful house and nice friends."

"Oh, you're too kind." Norman smiled. "Lucky that we keep running into each other at the lake. But the weather's not been good the past few days. I'm hoping next week it'll be better. You two ever been sailing?"

John sighed. "Twice. But I just sat and did nothing for two hours."

"I've sailed, many times. But not in America. Before I came here."

Curiosity crossed Norman's face. "Oh yeah? Where at?"

"In the Mediterranean. We lived in a village right on the water, a little bit south of Gaza City," explained Sammy. "My father was a fisherman and I used to sail with him. Two or three times a week. It was fun; I love to sail."

"Would the two of you like to go out sailing with me?" asked Norman. "I'm going on a trip to Michigan next Saturday, across the lake to Saugatuck. It's a whole day's trip. If you're interested, you're welcome to join."

Sammy looked at John with a shrug. "Next weekend sounds good to me. I'd like that." Seeing the expression on John's face, Sammy asked, "What's wrong?"

"I'm… I'm worried I'll get seasick. I'm not used to long sailing trips. It… scares me to go across the lake in a small boat."

Norman chuckled. "The boat's very safe. It's a thirty-two-footer. It's not that small. Very stable. Jeffrey's coming as well; you've met him, I think."

"Yes, Jeffrey." Sammy nodded. "We've met. His office is close to mine. We run into each other once in a while."

"We're meeting at the boat at Belmont Harbor at the crack of dawn, so around 5:30. If you prefer, you could stay overnight on the boat to make it easier on everyone. The boat's name is *Esperanza*. It's at the north end of the harbor on the east side, a few slips in. I'll be there Friday night around 9:00."

"Should we bring anything?" asked John. "Food? Drinks?"

"Whatever you like," replied Norman, obviously pleased they were coming. "We'll have breakfast and lunch, maybe dinner. The trip is about twelve hours long. Of course, bring a change of clothes."

They chatted about the trip for a while longer before others entered the conversation. Slowly, the discussion turned to the challenges of the HIV and AIDs crises.

Still, Sammy had a nice time, and he and John eventually left for John's apartment sometime just after midnight.

The following afternoon when Sammy got home, he found Michael working in the garden. It was cloudy with a threat of rain. As Sammy helped Michael pick up weeds, Michael asked, "So, how's your boyfriend?"

Sammy smiled at him. "We're not there yet. We're just dating. It sounds strange to me when you say 'boyfriend.' Actually, it scares me. I like John—a lot. But I'm not sure of anything." He glanced at him. "How's Patrick?"

"Oh, he's doing well. We talk on the phone every day. He's coming to Chicago next weekend. Maybe the three of us will have dinner together. You should invite John!"

"No, next weekend we're going sailing with Norman to Michigan. Norman's party was nice. I wish you could have been there. We had a great time."

There was a short stint of silence between them before Michael said, "I'm dating Patrick now."

"I kind of suspected that," Sammy replied.

Drops of rain splattered around them, and together, they decided to leave the weeds for another day.

Sammy mentioned writing letters to his family. "I told you about that guy I flirted with when we were kids, the one who's engaged to my sister now?"

"Yeah."

"I hope he's a straight man now."

"He might be a straight man. Maybe he was just experimenting with you. When I was in the Middle East, I noticed that there was no separate community of gay or straight men. It was all blended into society. It used to be that way in America, a long time ago, but things have changed. To tell you the truth, I'm not sure which is better. At times, I don't think we need labels. Why should people be defined by their sexuality? It's one part of who we are. It doesn't define our personality. I wonder sometimes if labeling increases discrimination. But I know we need that for legal protection." Michael sighed. "Eventually, I hope that when we achieve equal rights for the homosexual community, labels will just disappear."

"I'm not sure," mused Sammy. "All I know is I am not comfortable being labeled. I think it is my Middle Eastern background."

"I understand that."

Sammy excused himself to his room where he pondered on what he should write to his mother. He knew she was probably lonely, especially since the passing of her husband. But he didn't know what to say; he could share very little of his life with her.

He started to write, scratched it out, crushed the paper, and threw it in the garbage—again and again. Finally, he ended up with a brief letter describing his job and assuring her that he was healthy.

Sammy and Michael had a quiet Sunday. They spent the evening cooking, talking, and listening to music. The week went smoothly until Thursday when Sammy decided to go out for lunch to a small

Italian restaurant with Sue. At the restaurant, he ran into Jeffrey, who happened to be sitting at the table next to them with a friend.

Sammy hid his discomfort, as he worried Jeffrey would intentionally—or unintentionally—out him to Sue.

"You and John ready for Saturday's boat trip?" asked Jeffrey, his voice friendly and light.

"Yes, I'm ready. I'll be there tomorrow night. We're looking forward to it," Sammy replied.

"Oh, you're going on a boat trip?" asked Sue, intrigued.

"Sailing," Jeffrey explained.

"You're braver than me. I'm scared of the water," Sue continued.

Jeffrey and his friend paid their bill, bid them goodbye, and left.

"How do you know him?" Sue asked.

"I met him at a friend's party a while ago. I've seen him around here but never talked," replied Sammy. After that, the conversation returned to light-hearted matters, and Sue didn't probe further.

Sammy and John met Friday after work, packed, and headed for the marina. On the way, they picked up beer and food. Locating the boat was easy as it was the only one sporting a rainbow flag. Norman and Jeffrey were already present.

Norman assigned them the front bedroom, reserving the captain's room for himself and Jeffrey. He lit a kerosene lamp inside the boat, explaining, "It takes the humidity out and creates a nice atmosphere."

The four of them sat on the boat and drank. The evening was pleasant and the sky clear with a full moon and bright stars. The only disturbance was the noise from the cars that passed along Lake Shore Drive.

That night, neither Sammy nor John slept well due to the new environment and sounds. At 5:30, *Esperanza* pulled out of the harbor en route to Saugatuck, sails up and engines going. The sunrise was spectacular. The sun shone on the lake, illuminating golden waves that rippled outward from the bow of the boat. Chicago buildings gleamed in the dawn light, and seagulls flew overhead. Sammy was mesmerized by the beauty of it all.

As they churned farther out, the landscape grew quieter. The noise of the city disappeared, as well as the shoreline. Only the sound of the engines and the water lapping on the boat could be heard. Eventually, Norman quieted the engines and relied only on the sails.

Sammy helped with the rigging and steered the boat. He was thrilled with the opportunity to sail again. It reminded him of home and of his father. His glee was evident by the broad smile on his face.

Sailing in Gaza had been very basic with no high-tech instruments available. Sammy and his family had sailed using skill and knowledge. So he was excited to learn about instruments and modern sailing techniques from Norman.

Later that morning, Sammy found the opportunity to tell Jeffrey that he hadn't come out yet at work and that he'd like to keep it that way for now. Jeffrey gladly agreed.

The day passed pleasantly. They exchanged varying degrees of small talk and ate and drank in the shade. Around 4:00 in the afternoon, a shoreline began to appear, and they cheered. "That's Saugatuck," Norman announced. "I mark it with that hill over there."

They entered from the mouth of the Kalamazoo River. The view was magnificent. Beautiful homes met a pristine shoreline and enormous trees rose to meet the blue and pink sky. As they passed other boats, they exchanged waves.

Once the marina was in sight, Norman took down the sails and motored in. "Smooth sailing," he said. "The lake was flat and the wind was just right. Not a cloud in the sky. What a beautiful passage. One of the most beautiful I've seen. Cheers!"

They went out for dinner that night and then ventured into a dance club. Norman reminded them not to stay out too late as they had a long trip back the following day.

It was well after midnight by the time everyone made it back to *Esperanza*. Sammy and John couldn't be in the same bed without having sex. That night, they slept well.

They were underway once more by 8:00 the next morning. The lake was flat with a few, low-hanging clouds in the sky. It was much cooler than the previous day with temperatures hanging around 55 degrees.

A few hours in, the skies became overcast, prompting Norman to say, "It is a warm mass of air meeting a cold one. We might encounter some rain, but it doesn't look like it'll be a big deal."

Within the hour, the wind grew in strength and the lake became choppy with whitecaps. The boat rocked, tipping from side to side. Sammy suggested pulling the jib down and sailing only with the main, to which Norman agreed. It reduced some of the heeling.

As the sky grew darker, clouds gathered and the wind increased. Though Norman kept an even tone, he looked anxious.

The waves grew higher and rushes of water spilled across the deck. Lightning streaked across the sky as thunder pealed across the horizon into the clouds overhead. When a gust of wind caught the main sail and tipped the boat dangerously to one side, Sammy suggested they bring the sail in and only utilize the engine. Norman readily agreed and they worked together to reel the sail in under heavy rain.

Growing too anxious, John stood to take shelter in the cabin but lost his footing as the boat pitched starboard. With a shout, he toppled into the water.

Sammy called out as Norman threw John a life ring and began to turn the boat around. Before the boat had even slowed, Sammy leaped overboard and swam to John. Sammy gave John a quick hug to impart some calm to him and then tread water beside him. Norman and Jeffrey pulled them, shivering, back into the boat.

The rain came in great sheets as lightning continued to arc across the sky. With the engines going full tilt against the waves, the four disappeared inside the cabin to get dried off. Sammy checked on John who, despite his attempts to sound calm, was obviously shaken from the event.

The rest of the trip was quiet save the sound of thunder and the heavy rain on the deck. Only an hour prior to their arrival in Chicago did the weather improve and the Chicago skyline appear. They arrived at Belmont Harbor after 10:00.

Once back at John's apartment, John suggested that they have some warm tea. Sitting on the couch sipping their soothing beverages, John said, "Thank you for jumping in after me." He smiled. "You know, we both could have drowned."

"I'm an excellent swimmer. I wouldn't have let you drown," Sammy replied, cocky.

John held his gaze for a long moment, his eyes soft, and then leaned in and kissed him. "I want to… confess something," he said after a moment. "I think what I feel for you is more than just liking. I think I love you."

Sammy grinned. "I love you too."

Lost in John's embrace, Sammy sunk into the sweet bliss of unconditional love.

The next morning, they decided unanimously to call in sick and stay home. They spent the day sharing their dreams of a future together until finally, later that afternoon, Sammy had to leave.

On the way home, he thought of the drastic delineation his life had taken and how that change had altered how he thought and behaved. A little over two months ago, he would never have considered a relationship with a man. But now, it was his reality. His sweet, sweet reality.

CHAPTER 16

SAMMY BEGAN STAYING A FEW nights a week at John's home. On the weekends, John stayed with Sammy. The arrangement was a pleasant one, and Sammy found himself settling into the routine comfortably.

A few weeks passed. The Saturday on which Sammy was to escort Sue to her friend's wedding arrived. He wanted to look his best and so dressed in an elegant black suit with gleaming black shoes. After checking himself several times in the mirror, he left to pick up Sue.

Like Sammy, Sue was dressed nicely in a black, strapless dress. She wore a gold-and-diamond necklace, bracelet, and earring set. To Sammy, she looked like a movie star.

Sue took Sammy's arm, and they entered the hotel as if they were a celebrity couple. The reception room was vast and dripped with wealth. During cocktail hour, Sammy ordered his favorite drink and mingled with other guests alongside Sue. She knew a few people there and so introduced Sammy to friends and the bride's parents.

"This is Sammy. He's a friend and coworker," Sue said. "And this is Mr. and Mrs. Johnson."

Sammy visited, keeping in mind Michael's words of advice when it came to polite conversation. A friend of Mr. Johnson joined them shortly thereafter and was introduced as Mr. Marvin Cohen.

Upon hearing the name, Sammy flushed but tried to hide his discomfort. He *knew* that name. He *knew* that voice. He had heard it on the answering machine at John's apartment.

"Sammy, hm?" asked Mr. Cohen. "You have an accent. Where are you from?"

Sammy answered reluctantly, "I am Palestinian." He wished desperately for the earth to split open and swallow him whole at that moment.

"Oh. And what do you do?"

"I'm an accountant."

As Mr. Cohen probed, asking seemingly innocent questions, Sammy tried to keep himself from squirming. He was sure this man knew who he was. He was his son's lover.

Eventually, Sammy excused himself. He made a beeline for the bathroom, intent on escaping the situation. Once he was in the safety of the bathroom, he sighed and walked to a urinal. Upon hearing someone enter, he looked to find Mr. Cohen standing near the sinks. "Do you know John?" the man asked.

Sammy thought about lying but simply said, "Yes, I know John. And… you're his father, right?" He tried to cut through the tension. "You look alike."

Mr. Cohen didn't appear amused. "How well do you know him? Do you still see him regularly?"

"Look, I'd just like to use the restroom if that's okay…"

"Do you still see him regularly?" Mr. Cohen pressed.

Sammy met his gaze. "Yes. I still see John regularly. About how well I know your son… I don't know. But I think I know him well enough to love him."

A deep frown formed on Mr. Cohen's face. "He's not right for you, nor are you the right person for him."

"Right." Sammy excused himself and slipped out of the bathroom, disturbed. He found Sue and sat at their assigned table. Of course, Mr. Cohen and his date, Linda, were seated a single table away. Holding his head, Sammy said, "I'm kind of not feeling well. My head's hurting. Probably from the alcohol and the noise." He could feel Mr. Cohen's gaze on him.

"Do you want to leave?" asked Sue with real concern.

Deciding he needed to stay for her, Sammy replied, "I'll push through. If it gets worse, I'll let you know."

The night went on. Once the bride and groom entered, dinner was served. The band played music and some people started to dance.

After they finished their meal, Sue asked Sammy if he felt well enough to dance. He agreed. Mr. Cohen and his date, Linda, also began dancing nearby. Sue must have seen the looks he was throwing Sammy because she leaned in and asked, "What's wrong with this guy? Why's he looking at you like that? Do you know him?"

Sammy tried to keep calm. "This is the first time I've met him, but you know people. Maybe it's just our chemistry and he doesn't like me. Or maybe… it's because I'm Palestinian and he's Jewish."

Sue sighed in disgust. "Ignore him. Some people cannot get over their prejudices and hatred."

Mr. Cohen and Linda swept closer briefly, allowing John's father to mutter, "Stay away from him. Got it?"

Sammy ignored him and passed a lighthearted smile to Sue, who seemed worried. Both couples had returned to their respective tables when a friend came over to ask Sue for the next dance. Imparting Sammy a cheesy smile, she hurried off. Sipping water and sitting alone, Samme surveyed the dance floor.

"What's between you and John is pure lust," Mr. Cohen said over his shoulder. Sammy didn't look at him. "A relationship takes more than that. It takes understanding and having things in common. You should belong to the same culture. We're completely different."

Still, Sammy refused to look at him, feigning as if he couldn't hear him for the loud, booming music.

"We're enemies. I don't trust you. John is my only son, and I will protect him any way I can."

Deciding that he wouldn't allow threats to go unchallenged, Sammy whirled on him. "Mr. Cohen, I love your son. I know we are enemies, but don't you think it's time we changed that? Don't you think it's been long enough? You're protecting your son?" Sammy shook his head. "You're hurting him. You're teaching him distrust and bigotry." He held Mr. Cohen's gaze. "It's not your decision whether we stay together; it's hardly even my decision. It's John's decision."

Mr. Cohen's face turned red. "I'll make sure he tells you so. He's got to wake up. He's being blinded by lust."

Sammy nodded to him. "Yeah, good luck with that."

He was relieved when Sue finally declared it was time to leave an hour or two later. As she happily gabbed about the wedding and all that she'd seen and done, Sammy mused over his conversation with John's father.

Mr. Cohen had threatened him. He had said he would do anything to protect his son. What did that mean? Sammy considered whether he should tell John.

Sammy dropped Sue off at her apartment, waiting outside until she entered the building safely, and then went for a long drive along the lakeshore. It was shortly after 11:00. Despite the moonlight reflecting on the water of Lake Michigan, he couldn't get himself to calm down. After pulling onto a side street, he stopped at a phone booth and called John. It was almost midnight.

"Hello?" John's voice was drowsy.

"Hey, sorry," replied Sammy. "Sorry to wake you up."

When John next spoke, he sounded more awake and concerned. "What's going on? Are you okay?"

"Yeah, I just don't want to go home. I'm, uh, not far from your apartment right now. Could I come over?"

"Yeah, sure. Is everything okay?"

"Yeah, I'll see you soon."

John greeted him at the door with a concerned hug. "Hey, you okay?"

"Yeah, I'm fine. Just tired. I'll tell you about it in the morning," replied Sammy, relieved to be in his presence. John held him close all night.

The phone ringing woke them the following morning. Hearing the seriousness in John's voice, Sammy sat up and listened, knowing exactly who was on the other line. John's responses were short but light. It was obvious he was trying to sound unbothered. When he hung up, he turned to look at Sammy. "So, you met my father last night. Why didn't you tell me?"

"I was waiting until this morning," Sammy replied. "I didn't know how to handle it." He met John's gaze. "He was not nice to me. He told me to stay away from you."

John sat on the edge of the bed. "He's asked me to do the same. Look, let's not listen to what he has to say. We'll do whatever we want." When Sammy didn't respond, John asked, "What?"

"You don't understand. He said he will do *anything* to protect you. It sounded… like a threat. What will he do to me if I don't stay away from you? I'm… concerned. I'm not sure if he's bluffing."

"Calm down," cooed John. "He's not going to hurt you. I will make sure of that. I love you, Sammy, and I will not let anyone harm you, not even my father." John rolled across the bed to him and hugged him hard, kissing his face.

They spent the day together, walking through the park and along the water and watching the birds. John suggested that before summer ended they go camping not far from Saugatuck. Sammy agreed. So they decided to leave work early the next Friday and go camping, weather permitting.

"I have a tent and a sleeping bag that is big enough for the both of us," John explained. "We don't need much. It's just for two days."

They spent more time planning before Sammy lamented the fact that he had to go home. He spent the majority of the drive mulling over everything with John's father and the complexities of dating interculturally. To some extent, he understood Mr. Cohen's concerns, but the bigotry, the suspicion, the inherent racism—all of it had to stop.

Sammy wondered if Mr. Cohen just hadn't accepted the fact that John was gay. He couldn't understand the man's intentions. Love was simple. Two people in love with each other should be together regardless of race, religion, ethnicity, sex, or culture. Life with John made love simple. John couldn't help being Jewish just like Sammy couldn't change being born Palestinian. God wanted them to be the way that they were; God wanted them to meet.

Sammy scoffed as he thought about God. Who was he kidding? God didn't approve of him or his lifestyle. God shouldn't be brought into such conversation. Sammy had violated almost every Islamic religious rule that had been taught to him and that he believed. But still...

Perhaps God was much bigger than all of that. He knew everything; He understood everything. And Sammy still believed in Him and trusted Him. If God disapproved of Sammy's lifestyle and identity, then He wouldn't have made him that way. He was the one who could change Sammy; He could have changed Sammy had He wanted.

Sammy found Michael sitting at the kitchen table working on a crossword puzzle. They greeted each other warmly with a hug before Sammy launched into all that had transpired.

"Don't take John's father's words too seriously," Michael advised. "I'm sure it made you uncomfortable, but your relationship is with John. Not his father."

"Yeah, I guess. It's still worrying though," Sammy murmured. Looking to change the topic, he asked about Patrick.

"I had a wonderful time in Milwaukee. I think…" Michael grinned. "I think I'm falling in love with Patrick. I like him very much. We have so much in common, and Milwaukee's not far. I could see him every weekend. One weekend he'll come here, and then the next, I'll go there."

Sammy was overjoyed to hear this as it had been well over two years since Joseph's passing. Of course, his roommate wasn't over the much-loved man, but Sammy was greatly pleased to hear that his heart had healed. Joseph would always be with Michael because he was a part of him.

CHAPTER 17

Sammy and John met the following weekend and packed up to go camping. They were excited by the prospect of embarking on a new adventure, just the two of them. The campground was two and a half hours from Chicago, the destination a popular one among gay men. This was made obvious as traffic became worse the closer they drew. The last weekend in August was hot and the air still.

Once inside the campground, they lined up behind a slew of other cars to wait for their turn to check in. Most of the cars' occupants were couples, primarily men, though there were groups of friends present as well. Excitement was in the air and laughter drifted on the wind.

After they were assigned a campsite, they put up their tent. It was a small area, clear of any growth and surrounded by thick trees and heavy foliage. They spent time organizing the tent and then rested briefly before going for a walk at sunset. The evening was spectacular. Fiery red clouds peered down upon soft, white sand as a light breeze brushed the water. The sun watched them hold one another, listened to their hearts beat, and reflected itself in their eyes as though it could see what they saw in each other.

Romance, love, and beauty were all around. Only the pleasant sound of the waves brushing the beach and birds twittering overhead punctured the peace.

Amid the magical atmosphere were Sammy and John, lost in each other's presence and comfort. That night, they made love time and time again.

The following morning, they went fishing but didn't have much luck. "Here's lunch," John jokingly announced, grimacing at his still-bare lure. "We're not going to eat."

"Let's go to another area. Maybe we'll have better luck elsewhere."

As they walked along the beach, a group of men approached from the opposite direction. Once they drew closer, one of the men yelled, "Ezra! Ezra!"

Sammy glanced over his shoulder to make sure that the man was addressing him and John and then looked at John, bewildered.

"Mark!" John called, surprised. "What on earth has brought you to this part of the world? I thought you settled down in Israel!"

Mark and John greeted each other casually as the others hung back. Sammy stayed close to John, purposefully keeping his face devoid of emotion.

"No, I live in Chicago now. I just moved back a month ago. Actually, I was going to give you a call!"

Smiling, John turned to Sammy. "This is my friend Sammy. He's Palestinian."

Mark looked between them, obviously at a loss as to how to respond. But John seemed to have expected this reaction because he quickly directed the conversation elsewhere. Eventually, they bid each other farewell, and the group of young men meandered off, laughing and talking.

"Did Mark forget your name?" asked Sammy softly, watching them.

John chuckled. "No, my name is Ezra. My father wanted to call me Ezra, but my mother wanted my name to be John. I was called Ezra for a long time, especially when I went to Israel."

Sammy met his gaze, alarmed. "You went to Israel? You never told me about that. When? How long ago?"

"Oh, a long time ago. I was in high school when my father insisted that I go to Israel with a group of Jewish students. We went to a school about twenty kilometers north of Tel Aviv. That's where I met Mark. He always calls me Ezra; it's my Jewish name."

They continued walking.

"My experience was interesting," John said. "Spiritual and somewhat religious. I felt some connection to Israel, but it's not a place I would choose to live. I was very uncomfortable with the inhumane and brutal treatment of Palestinians by the Israeli government and army. I was totally against it then, and I still am. Honestly, despite the antisemitism here, I feel very much American."

Sammy hesitantly asked, "I assume you visited Jaffa?" He was still disturbed that John had hidden such a trip from him.

John nodded. "I did. I visited your parents' hometown. Maybe someday we'll go together to visit."

"We could do that," Sammy replied. "You'd be allowed to live there if you wanted; you'd be welcomed with open arms. But I would not. Imagine that."

"Well, according to Jewish law, I'm not Jewish either. My father and grandfather insisted we be raised Jewish. I told you. I was sent to a synagogue and converted. All of that. My mother wasn't very happy."

They forgot about fishing and sat to talk on the beach. There were more important matters to attend to than a lakeside hobby.

Identity, culture, heritage, religion. They were different in so many ways but similar in others. What issues could they talk about? What issues should they avoid? What had the potential to bring them together? Likewise, what had the power to tear them apart—for good?

"Everyone calls you John," Sammy mused. "You don't use the name Ezra anymore. Why?"

John smiled sadly. "It makes life easier for me. Though the law firm I work at is run largely by Jewish managers, our clients are not. I've heard how people talk about Jews, not knowing that I am one. Their remarks aren't exactly flattering. There are so many people who are antisemitic; they hate Jews. There is still tremendous prejudice in this country against Jews. Maybe not on the surface, maybe not in the government, but for sure in people's behaviors and in how they perceive us."

"So, you're denying yourself, your heritage, and identity, because of people's ignorance?" asked Sammy, keeping his voice even. He didn't want John to hear how upset he was. "I refuse to do that. I used to do that, but not anymore. It made me feel awful. People will make remarks and they will hate me for where I come from, but that's not my problem. It's their problem."

John nodded thoughtfully before silence fell over them. Eventually, he said, "So, fishing?"

Sammy shrugged. "A walk sounds better to me. I'm getting hungry too. You?"

"Why don't we eat and then go for a walk in the woods?" John suggested.

They returned to their campsite, jumped in the car, and drove to the nearest town, about five miles away. The food at the nondescript and bland restaurant they visited was forgetful, prompting John to promise a better dinner that night.

Afterward, they ventured deep into the forest until they reached a creek surrounded by overgrown vines. They sat in the shade of a grapevine in near silence except for the birds singing and the rustling of leaves. When movement caught their attention, they found a stray cat.

The gray tabby approached them comfortably and rubbed against John's legs, meowing. The tabby didn't look healthy. Its coat was matted and its eyes cloudy. They chuckled and lavished attention on the feline until it walked away—and then returned with four kittens, all mewing hungrily.

"Shall we bring them some food?" John asked. "We have cold meat in the cooler."

They went back to camp and retrieved food, but the cat refused to eat it. The mother was too sick, and the kittens weren't old enough for solid food. Sammy suggested that they drive to town for kitten formula.

They bought kitten formula at a pet store and returned to feed the starving balls of fluff. They ate as though they had never eaten before. Sammy became concerned when the mother cat refused the cat food they had also purchased. He and John sat with the cats for well over an hour trying to get close enough to the kittens to grab them, but they kept scampering away. Meanwhile, the mother cat remained stretched out under the grape vines, not moving, staring at Sammy and John with clouded eyes.

Eventually, they had to give up on their venture and return to their campsite. They went to dinner that night and talked of nothing but the cats. Sammy was relieved when John agreed to go visit the feline family first thing the following morning.

The mother cat was dead. They found her lifeless body among the grape vines. Her hungry, meowing kittens ambushed them the moment they entered the area. Quickly, Sammy and John dished out kitten formula and contemplated what to next do. If they left now, the kittens would die.

After some discussion, they buried the mother cat under the grape vines, collected the feisty kittens, and headed back to camp. Sammy didn't have experience taking care of cats, and neither did John. Thus, transporting them to Chicago became quite an ordeal. The car needed a good cleaning after the adventure. But the kittens were cute and painfully in need of looking after.

Once at John's apartment, Sammy called Michael to ask for advice.

"Bring them home," Michael said, perhaps a little too quickly. "We'll take care of them."

All attention turned to how best to tend to the kittens. Sammy made a nest of blankets for them in the basement of his house while Michael set up a litter box. John helped in feeding and grooming the kittens. Between the three of them, they figured they equaled one good mother cat.

They eventually decided on Moses and Hasaan for the two male kittens and Mariam and Fatima for the two females, a good compromise, Sammy thought.

When caring for the four young kittens became too much, Sammy and John decided to split the litter between their homes to provide better one-on-one care.

"I received a call from Kris," said Michael one evening as he joined Sammy on the back porch. "You know, the woman we met at Jim's party. She's having a pool party at her house and wanted to invite us."

"When is it?"

Michael flashed a smile. "This Sunday. She said you could bring your significant other."

On Sunday, Sammy, John, Michael, and Patrick drove to Kris' house together. It was an elegant and large home located in one of the wealthiest neighborhoods in the area. Cars lined both sides of the street.

A diverse mixture of straight and gay men and women were in attendance. A large, deep pool with a sizeable diving board and a vast covered patio took up most of the backyard. Already, guests were enthusiastically swimming. Beside the pool was an outdoor shower and changing room where Sammy and John dressed in their swimsuits.

With a grimace, Sammy admitted, "I forgot my towel."

"Oh, no problem," replied John. "I'll share. As a matter of fact, this towel was given to me by my grandmother for my bar mitzvah."

They mingled with the others for a short while before temptation called; Sammy jumped into the pool followed by John. The evening was pleasant and the water cool but not chilly.

"Do you know how to dive?" asked John teasingly.

"I actually did some diving in college," replied Sammy.

"Oh, did you now?" John laughed.

"No, really. I took a diving class." Sammy clambered out of the pool, strode over to the diving board, and gracefully dove back into the pool. It was a good dive with a little splash on the entry. When he got out and approached the diving board again, people paused in their activities to watch. Another excellent dive.

Grinning and in love with the positive attention, Sammy decided to try a dive that was a little more complex, one that incorporated a backward spin. He bounced twice, arms overhead, and then leaped. His form was precise but he realized, belatedly, that he had not pushed off far enough from the board.

John gasped as he saw Sammy's head smack the edge of the board. Blood spewed in an arc as Sammy toppled into the water, unconscious. Frantic, John—and a few others—powered toward Sammy's limp body as it sank beneath the water. With two others' help, John struggled to pull Sammy upward. Other partygoers waiting along the poolside drew Sammy over the lip of the pool.

Panting, John heaved himself out and fell on Sammy, his hands shaking. "Sammy, Sammy," he wheezed, touching his face. He didn't know what to do.

From behind him, he heard someone direct another to call 911.

Everything happened in a blur. It took but a few minutes for an ambulance to arrive. Though John and other partygoers had managed to stop the bleeding with pressure and gauze, Sammy had yet to awaken.

Seated beside Sammy in the ambulance, John peered at him from over cold fingertips. EMTs worked on him diligently, calmly, taking vitals, examining his limp body, and inserting IV fluids. Halfway to the hospital, Sammy woke but remained dazed.

Once at the facility, the EMTs rushed Sammy into the emergency department with John behind them. Hospital personnel requested that he stay in the waiting room as doctors worked on Sammy. In shock, John shuffled to the waiting room and sat for a few minutes, his mind reviewing the incident again and again.

Eventually, he decided he needed to call Michael, who immediately came to the hospital with Patrick in tow.

The wait was excruciating. Even though he checked with the front desk staff periodically, no word on Sammy's status filtered to the waiting room. Finally, a couple of hours later, a nurse came out, beckoning to them.

She led them to a room farther in the hospital where John found Sammy conscious but weary. Tears spilling down his cheeks, John grasped Sammy's hand and rubbed his arm lovingly. Sammy looked at him, not fully lucid.

The diagnosis was in—a concussion, a bad one. The hospital was going to keep Sammy for observation for a few days. Sammy was assigned a room in the hospital, and John stayed with him, holding his hand until he went to sleep, which was often.

Monday, Labor Day, came. John sat with Michael in Sammy's room, waiting, as Sammy had been taken for x-rays at 9:00. When he didn't return after half an hour, John grew anxious. Surely x-rays didn't take *that* long.

Sammy was returned to the room an hour later, his skin pale and eyes unfocused. He didn't look good nor was he responding. The nurse asked John and Michael to leave the room as doctors entered.

Heart sinking, John trailed after Michael into the hallway. Michael placed an arm around John and guided him to the waiting room. Sometime later, a doctor collected them, drawing them back into Sammy's room for what seemed to be a solemn conversation.

"There's been internal bleeding," the doctor explained. "It's serious. Uh, we're doing everything we can right now. But the next few days are crucial."

John buried his face in his hands as tears came.

"Does he have any family nearby? Anyone we can call?" the doctor continued.

"He doesn't have any blood relatives in the U.S.," Michael grimly replied. "We're his family."

"What can we do?" whispered John, his gaze set on Sammy who was asleep. "Is there anything? We'll do anything."

The doctor nodded, grave. "Prayers, lots of prayers. These next few days are going to be hard."

John left that afternoon to go home. On the way, he stopped at a mosque, then at a synagogue, and then at a church. In the evening, he drove back to the hospital and sat with Sammy for a few hours, holding his hand.

John was dismayed the following day to find no difference in Sammy's state. When awake, Sammy was semi-lucid and gripped John's hand periodically, but for the most part, he slept.

That evening, his coworker Sue came to visit. She introduced herself as Sammy's friend and touched him fondly as she spoke to him. She eventually seated herself nearby and chatted with John about all that had transpired.

Uncaring that Sue saw, John took Sammy's hand and squeezed it as he spoke. He stumbled to a stop mid-sentence when Sammy suddenly squeezed it back. John stood, his eyes searching Sammy's face.

Sammy slowly looked up at him. "Hi, John…" he murmured frailly.

John couldn't help the sob of relief that escaped him as he leaned forward and kissed Sammy's cheek adoringly. "Oh, I love you."

"Love you… too," Sammy managed.

John caressed his face and kept a tight grip on his hand. "Sue's here too. You know Sue, right?"

Sammy searched the room before his gaze settled on Sue. "Yeah."

Sue joined John at Sammy's bedside and stroked his arm. "I'm glad to see you awake, friend." She smiled at him. "Everyone at work has been worried."

Sammy tried to nod but the motion made him grimace. He closed his eyes, weak.

"I'll leave you two alone." She gave Sammy a fond pat. "Hang in there, Sammy."

CHAPTER 18

Sammy's health improved rapidly. In four days, he was out of the hospital and back at work. But he wasn't the same. Most of the time, he kept to himself. He didn't interact often with his coworkers as he became grossly concerned about being outed as gay.

Sue visited with him often and eventually said, "You've been kind of distant since the accident. Are you feeling well?"

Sammy pondered on the question for a moment. "Physically, I'm fine. I'm just… worried."

"About?"

He glanced at her and then lowered his voice. John had told him that she had seen their interactions in the hospital. "About everyone finding out about…" He gestured to himself.

"I haven't told anyone," Sue asserted. "You decide to be out or not."

"Oh…" He smiled. "Thank you, Sue."

Despite feeling relieved, he remained generally unhappy. Everything seemed complicated. His relationship with John, work, his relationship with his coworkers… It was all exhausting.

On the way home from work one afternoon, Sammy contemplated whether being gay and having to hide his relationship with John was going to be a lifelong struggle. Would he always have to pretend to be something he wasn't? He had been comfortable with the natural contradictions of his life before John; now though, he couldn't bear to continue hiding everything.

At home, he found Michael cooking dinner for them. Sammy changed clothes and came back downstairs; he kept his hat on to cover his shaved head.

"You've seemed down," Michael remarked, not taking his gaze away from a pan. "Something going on between you and John?"

Sammy sighed. "No, not between us. It's me... Or maybe it's society as a whole. I don't know. I'm not sure of anything anymore." He slumped in his chair. "I'm afraid of being out, of being me. I've always lived a double life where very few people know about my lifestyle. And I was comfortable with that. But now... I'm close to coming out and that's making me... I don't like it."

"Because you don't know how others are going to behave or react?"

Sammy nodded. "It feels like I'm moving into another community or another country with no knowledge of it."

Michael gave Sammy a warm hug. "You're moving to another phase of your life. Change is difficult. But things will sort themselves out. Don't think too much on it."

"I'll try..."

Michael changed the subject. "I cooked you something nice tonight to lift your spirits. It's your mother's recipe for fish."

Sammy smiled. "I could smell it." He picked out a nice bottle of California white, and they ate a hearty meal with a side of nostalgia. "Next weekend is Rosh Hashanah. John's going to spend it with his grandparents. Maybe you and I should do something fun."

"Oh, we can go for a drive in Wisconsin to see the changing foliage. And then we can have lunch with Patrick on the way back," Michael suggested. Sammy agreed.

Sammy arrived at John's apartment the following morning at 7:00. He was surprised to find the apartment a mess and cat fur everywhere—on the furniture, drifting around the kitchen, on John. "Enjoying your new pets?" asked Sammy, amused.

"I am, but they're... a lot. I don't know how to take care of cats. But you know what? My father's girlfriend says she can take care of one. So, that'll make it easier."

They called in an order from a Middle Eastern restaurant that John often raved about and waited for it to be delivered, during which time, John recommended that they do something fun.

Half an hour later, the doorbell to his apartment rang. They were both naked in bed. John jumped up, put on his robe, and answered the door.

Sammy set up plates and opened a bottle of wine, and they ate at the table with the two kittens mewing beneath them. Midway through dinner, the phone rang. It was John's grandmother.

"I'll call you back later. I have a friend over for dinner." Returning to the table, John explained, "My grandparents are coming to town to stay with my father. They do it every year. This is the year 5752 on the Jewish calendar, did you know?"

"How do you celebrate Rosh Hashanah?"

"Oh, we go to the synagogue. On the second day, we have a habit of visiting a small river that's a few blocks from my father's house, and we empty our pockets of breadcrumbs. Basically, it means we get rid of all our sins, and the ducks enjoy it. It's a tradition. It makes my father and grandparents happy, so I go along with it. I don't really believe in anything called sin; that's nonsense. Today, I'm full of sins and tomorrow I'm sin-free? That's total bullshit."

Sammy grinned as Moses the kitten attempted to climb John's pants leg to the table.

On the way home that evening, Sammy thought about the recent onslaught of Judaism that seemed to be suddenly permeating John's life. His mentioning of his bar mitzvah, his name, Rosh Hashanah, and now his father and grandparents. He had also mentioned that Yom Kippur was approaching and after that Sukkot. There was a never-ending stream of Jewish holidays. And then after those, he would celebrate Christmas and Easter. Yet... he had not invited Sammy to join him on any of those holidays.

Of course, those weren't Sammy's holidays and they never would be. Sammy celebrated his holidays alone, sometimes with Michael, but mostly alone. And no one seemed to care. In fact, it had been many years since Sammy had actually celebrated a holiday as a Muslim.

While growing up in Gaza, his favorite time of year had been Ramadan, during which he had fasted and prayed. He had loved being surrounded by family and friends and going to the mosque with his father. He missed his mother's Ramadan table that used to be crowded with her special Ramadan recipes. Since arriving in America, he had left all of that behind. His culture, his heritage, his traditions and holidays.

Sammy's musings led him to a startling realization—he'd love to celebrate Rosh Hashanah with John, just to be with him. But that would never be possible given John's family. If Sammy weren't Palestinian or Muslim, would John feel more inclined to invite him? He felt excluded. Not that he would have gotten much from the celebrations since they weren't *his*. But still, being excluded hurt.

He felt excluded here in America.

He had felt excluded while back home in Gaza.

He no longer belonged to a group of people, a culture, a collective.

The day of Rosh Hashanah, Michael and Sammy went for a long drive in Wisconsin to view the changing fall foliage. Sammy stared absent-mindedly out the window, his mind everywhere and nowhere. Michael seemed to sense his restlessness and tried to distract him with remarks about the beauty of nature, but Sammy's attention remained short-lived.

Eventually, Michael turned their conversation onto their new relationships. He shared with Sammy his optimism for his relationship with Patrick, which Sammy was pleased to hear. As Michael explained some of his and Patrick's most recent squabbles and misunderstandings, Sammy tried to glean advice. But he knew his relationship with John was far more complex than the older men's. The cultural and religious differences between himself and John were far more difficult to navigate.

CHAPTER 19

John didn't see Sammy for a while as it was Rosh Hashanah and he was preoccupied with entertaining his family. Once his grandparents left, he finally found the time to take the female kitten to Linda.

As usual, he found his father and Linda watching television in the living room. Linda excitedly greeted him and cooed over the young cat as the feline regarded her from inside a box.

Linda immediately released the gray, who looked so much like her mother, and they watched as the newcomer explored the house with bold curiosity. John caught sight of his father watching, a slight smile on his face.

Linda set up food and water and a litter box in the laundry room as well as a pile of blankets as a bed. Eager to showcase the young cat's reflexes and playful nature, John retrieved the pink ball he had brought and rolled it across the floor. "Get it, Fatima," John encouraged, grinning. Linda squealed as the cat went scampering across the living room to tackle the toy.

"Fatima?" asked John's father.

Recognizing the tone, John just smiled. "Yeah. That's what we named her."

"That's an Arabic Muslim name. Do you know that, John?"

John acted indifferent. "I didn't know that, but it doesn't really matter."

"If she stays here, we will be changing her name. I'm sure your Palestinian friend selected that name… I can't believe you're still seeing him. I've asked you to stop this madness." His father's voice increased. "Those people can't be trusted."

Tired of arguing and of always having to find an excuse, John replied, "Call her whatever you want. A name is just a name. She's too young to recognize a name yet though. So it doesn't really matter."

"Oh, what about the name Sara?" asked Linda in an obvious attempt to break up the tension in the room. Both men agreed.

John left shortly thereafter, annoyed and more bothered than he cared to admit. His father's prejudice weighed heavily on his shoulders; he was so tired of having to carry it.

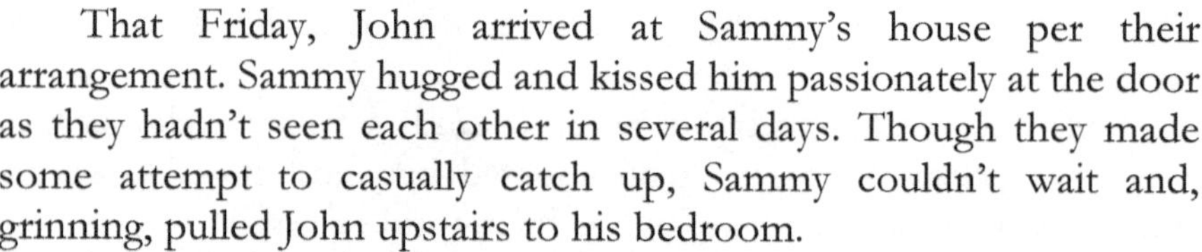

That Friday, John arrived at Sammy's house per their arrangement. Sammy hugged and kissed him passionately at the door as they hadn't seen each other in several days. Though they made some attempt to casually catch up, Sammy couldn't wait and, grinning, pulled John upstairs to his bedroom.

After vigorous adult activities, they took a shower and dressed.

"I'm hungry," Sammy said. "Let's go out somewhere we've never been."

"A French restaurant recently opened," offered John. "I think it's called La Brissori. Wanna try that?"

La Brissori was absolutely packed and boasted a 45-minute wait. With nothing better to do, they sat at the bar and sipped red wine. John motioned to a male patron across the bar, a sort of acknowledgment.

"You know him?" asked Sammy.

John nodded as the man made his way over to them. To Sammy, the newcomer didn't appear comfortable. "Sammy, this is David."

"Nice to meet you," Sammy politely greeted, but David remained awkward, refusing to look at Sammy. John exchanged some light-hearted chitchat with him before David and his partner were seated.

Sammy watched them go. "I don't think your friend liked me."

John chuckled. "Yeah, it wasn't you. I, uh, dated David for a couple of months and then I… broke up with him after I met you." Sammy looked at him in alarm. "It wasn't serious. I knew we weren't a good match. I was going to break it off with him anyway. But I'm sure he thinks you're the reason I broke up with him."

"Why'd you hide that from me?" asked Sammy.

"I wasn't hiding it. I just didn't think it was important."

"You broke up with someone because of me," Sammy argued.

"No, I always intended to break up with him. Were you listening to what I just said?"

Sammy remained aloof throughout dinner, his mind preoccupied. It was true. John hadn't hidden the information, but he hadn't readily offered it up either. Sammy tried not to let his insecurities get the best of him, but that was easier said than done. Of course, when John suggested that they go to a club, Sammy declined the invitation, citing fatigue.

At John's apartment, Sammy decided he'd rather go home. Although John tried to convince him to stay the night, Sammy insisted on leaving. In his stubborn, usual way, he left moodily.

Unsurprising, he found a message on his answering machine when he arrived home. Sammy listened as John explained that he never tried to hide anything from him and that Sammy was blowing things out of proportion.

Sammy retreated to his bedroom and lay down, his mind cloudy. When he couldn't sleep, he sat at his desk and started yet another letter to his mother to add to the collection of mail he never intended to send to her.

Dear Mother,

It is almost midnight, and I am unable to sleep. I think of you and of my brothers and sisters. I remember when you told me that you don't understand America or Americans. You're right. I don't understand them either. I'm a stranger here; I'm a stranger to myself.

There's no question that I feel part-American most of the time, but other times… I feel like an outsider. I like my sense of freedom here. America has given me many things that I would never have been allowed in Gaza—including John.

Mother, at times, I can't imagine myself without him. He's become such an important part of my life. I think of him all the time; I plan my life around him; I need to be with him. I'm in love with him. But whether we can live together, can be real partners together, is still a question. If you met him, you'd love him. But I'm sure you'd also hate him because he destroyed your dreams of me finding a wife and having children.

John made me want a completely different life than what you imagined for me. He's created for me family. Not one made of a man and woman, but of two men.

Mother, perhaps you think I am out of my mind. I thought that, too, when I first realized that I would like to have a man for a partner. But now… this is the only natural way for me. Of course, I worry if John is the right man for me. Most of the time, I feel that he is, but we often have problems communicating. Frequently, I don't understand him or his intentions. Maybe it's me. I constantly feel as though he's hiding things from me. But very likely, that is his way of communicating.

I have found that he does not tell me everything because, to him, not everything is important. In his mind, he thinks he is sharing with me what is necessary and relevant. But I often feel that there are things that I need to know, and he's just not telling me, like his history with David or his trip to Israel…

Sammy stopped writing, his pen motionless above the letter. His eyes focused on the wood grain of his desk. He so desperately wanted someone—anyone—to talk to.

A noise downstairs startled him from his thoughts. Michael was home. Deciding that he would continue later, Sammy left his thoughts and went to greet Michael.

"John upstairs?" asked Michael from the kitchen.

Sammy stood in the doorway. "No, I assume he's at home."

Michael looked back at him with an appraising glance. "Something going on?"

Sammy shrugged to make it seem unimportant, but when he met Michael's gaze he let his impassive façade fall.

They chatted for the next hour at the kitchen table. Sammy grew misty-eyed but managed to keep his emotions relatively in check as he listened to Michael. His roommate explained with sage wisdom that miscommunication occurred in relationships, straight and gay, new and old. He went on to assure him that just because John didn't share information, it didn't mean that he was purposefully hiding it.

Tired but feeling better, Sammy wearily regarded Michael. "Well, so, how's it going between you and Patrick?"

Michael chuckled. "I'm spending the weekend with Patrick in Milwaukee. The weather is supposed to be beautiful. We're going to have an Indian summer."

Sammy did his best to act interested in Michael's plans, but his mind whirred. Relationships weren't easy, that much Sammy now knew. Miscommunication was going to happen, according to Michael. It was how they navigated it that determined how the relationship would proceed.

Of course, that didn't please Sammy. He wanted to know everything about John. He wanted to know where he was, what he was doing, who he had been in the past, who he had dated, and where he went... All of it, past and present. Was that love? Sammy didn't know.

CHAPTER 20

SAMMY DECIDED NOT TO CALL John for a few days to clear his head. He picked up the phone a few times, the urge strong within him, but ultimately hung up. He needed time to think.

By Thursday, he could stand it no longer and dialed John around noon to invite him to lunch. To his great disappointment, John apologized, saying that he had a prior engagement. Clenching his jaws, Sammy fought the impulse to hang up. Was John seeing someone else? Or maybe John just didn't want to see him?

Later that evening, Sammy decided to go to the bars on Halsted Street by himself. He stopped a few times at phone booths to check his messages on his answering machine at home, hoping there would be a message from John. But John never called. After he had dinner at a small, local restaurant, he made his way to a piano bar where they played Broadway tunes. He didn't stay for long as he was beyond restless.

He wandered down to the club where he had first met John. He crossed the street and started down the sidewalk. Hearing the tone of a familiar voice, he looked ahead to find John and another man walking and talking.

Heart hammering, Sammy drew himself into the entrance of a building to remain unseen and watched as John and the other man entered the club. Sammy's heart hurt and he seethed with anger. He had been right to worry! But now he didn't know what to do. Should he go and confront John? Or should he avoid him and never talk to him again? Tears burned in his eyes as his cold fingers trembled.

Sammy returned to the piano bar and drank like he had never drank before.

He stayed until the bar closed. Completely intoxicated and unsteady on his feet, he staggered from the bar, intent on finding his car. It was shortly after 2:00 in the morning. The streets were mostly empty, save the few bar patrons who had been kicked out at closing.

Turned around and unsure of his surroundings, Sammy wandered listlessly, stumbling and mumbling to himself. When two men appeared in his periphery, he thought they were there to help him. Instead, they asked him for money. He gave them everything—his watch, necklace, ring, and wallet—but they wouldn't leave him alone. With sneers, they pushed him, causing his unsteady legs to collapse under him. Once on the ground, they kicked him and then, when that wasn't enough, beat him. People heard the ruckus and called the police.

A few minutes later, Sammy was picked up by an ambulance and taken to the hospital.

Though he had not incurred any serious physical wounds, he was devastated. Emotionally and mentally defeated, he felt broken, his soul violated. Nobody had gotten a good look at the assailants, not even Sammy. It had been dark, and he had been blackout drunk. They would never be caught.

Sammy was released from the hospital the following morning. By the time he had managed to find his car and get home, it was near noon. He spent the rest of the day in bed, crying and nursing his injuries. When Michael got home that night, Sammy revealed to him all that had transpired.

Seated beside him, a comforting arm wrapped around his shoulders, Michael suggested that Sammy confront John directly and ask him straight out about the man. Speculating and guessing was not going to do him any good.

"He left me a message," Sammy explained. "Yesterday afternoon. He told me a friend was visiting from out of town and that they would be going out, but he… never asked me to go with them."

"Sometimes that can be awkward," offered Michael. "If he's an old friend, he wants time to catch up and reminisce."

"I always feel so excluded."

"Sammy, like I said—don't speculate or build a narrative in your head about who the person is. If you had someone visiting from Gaza, would you immediately invite John with you to pick them up from the airport?"

Sammy shrugged, though he knew Michael was right.

"You need to talk with him."

Sammy tried several times to call John but found the action of holding the phone too difficult. Perhaps their relationship was over for good.

Determined to safeguard himself from the pain, he allowed thoughts of a life without John to overcome him. Perhaps it was time for a change, time to find new ways of living, new likes and dislikes, new dreams. Maybe John was the stepping stone to a life with someone else. Of course, dating a woman was now out of the question; that wasn't going to happen.

Or perhaps John was a warning. Maybe Sammy needed to buckle down and focus on his work. He could get a promotion, make more money, and get an apartment all his own. That scared him more than he cared to admit since he had never before lived by himself, but there was a first for everything. He'd find an apartment—not near Boystown—and strike out, alone. He was 28. He would face the world, surefooted and confident.

Michael and Joseph had gifted him a bracelet the day he arrived in America. The bracelet was simple and had "You have the right to be yourself, here and now" engraved on its band. It was time to heed that advice. It was time to turn his life around and change for the better.

Tomorrow, he would call John and end everything.

Filled with stubborn resolve, Sammy began to go through everything that John had given him—letters, notes, pictures, a dried rose—and stacked them in a little box. Wiping tears from his cheeks, he held one picture close to his heart in a silent goodbye and then placed it in the box.

The phone rang.

Sammy cleared his throat and answered.

"I called your work phone," said John in a huff, "but got told you were home, sick. Are you okay?"

"Yeah," Sammy mumbled. "Um, look, it's over."

"What? What is?"

"Us. I saw you the other night. With another man. I'm just… Yeah, it's over."

"Wait, wait, wait. Let me explain," stammered John.

"I don't want explanations, John. It was clear you didn't want me there. Um, I'm going to send all your stuff back to you—"

"Sammy!" John interrupted. "Let me explain. Do *not* hang up. I know you want to hang up, don't."

"Yeah." Sammy hung up.

After collecting everything, Sammy mailed the box of tokens to John from the post office and began looking for apartments. That evening after Michael came home, he explained to his roommate that everything was over and that Sammy was searching for a new place to live. The disappointment on Michael's face was evident.

Sammy went to work the next day, bewildered. Nothing looked the same. The weather had turned off cold; the sky was gray and threatened snow. At one time, he had seen the beauty of low-hanging clouds and barren trees. He had felt that God had accepted him and fulfilled his dreams, the spoken and the unspoken. He had sensed that God was okay with him being his truest self. Now, he hated his drive into the city.

But John had opened the door to his cage and freed him. He had unlocked his shackles and cut loose his chains. And for that, Sammy wholeheartedly appreciated John. He had helped him cast off filters through which he had perceived the world, permitting light and love to enter unimpeded.

Sammy felt like one large question mark, like a culmination of any number of contradictions. He both hated the world around him and loved the new person he had discovered within himself. He could see a future forming before him yet felt alone, intimidated by the monumental change taking place within him. Nevertheless, whatever world took shape, it would be his, and only his.

He had once run from everything, especially his feelings. But John had awakened his emotions and helped him identify those most burdensome. He had prompted Sammy to scrutinize and question the aspects of his life that irked him the most, like religion and culture. Ideas, concepts, and ways of living now had meaning and held significance.

Sammy grimaced in thought as one final contradiction formed in his mind. John.

If Sammy had evolved and developed so much under John's care... why was he leaving him? Why wasn't he giving him the benefit of the doubt? Why wasn't he working to understand all that John was?

Sammy's thoughts turned to John. Where was he? Was he at work? Was he by himself or perhaps he was with that "friend?" Was he happy?

Sammy pondered on the influence family and parents had over their children and wondered what type of effect John's father had on him. Michael's remark from the other day rang clear in his head. If one of Sammy's friends from Gaza landed in Chicago, would Sammy immediately invite John to go collect him from the airport? No, certainly not. Sammy would want to visit with the friend and reacclimate to their relationship before introducing his very American Jewish partner.

It was over, of that Sammy was certain, but he secretly wished it was not. He wanted to be strong, rational. He wanted to push John's handsome face from his mind, to act as though he had never met him. But that wasn't possible.

Love.

Sammy chided himself, as love and rationality did not go hand-in-hand. Therefore, one had to be dropped.

CHAPTER 21

A FEW DAYS PASSED. SAMMY ignored John's calls. Though he sincerely wanted to know who John had been hanging out with the previous week, Sammy stubbornly kept a lid on his heart and curiosity.

Upon returning from lunch one day, he found three emails waiting for him, all from John. He selected the email entitled "Very, Very Important," and read.

Sammy,

I want you to know one important thing: I never intended to hurt you or exclude you. You are an important person in my life and bring me so much joy and happiness.

I know I need to be a better communicator. I'm sorry for not sharing information openly. I swear I will do better in the future.

The person you saw me with the other night was a friend visiting from Tel Aviv. I was concerned about you being uncomfortable around him and his friends who were at the club. It would have been awkward had I invited you to come; I didn't want to put you in such an uncomfortable situation.

But when I was on the dance floor, your face never left my mind. I so wished you were with me. Honestly, I can't stop thinking about you. I miss you. Always. I promise to make it up to you.

We need to talk.

I want to spend the rest of my life with you. I want to be able to talk with you to resolve our disagreements. Yes, of course, we have our differences, but we can work through those. Like any other couple, we're going to agree and disagree on some things. That's normal in any relationship. So, let's make it happen.

I hate to see you hurting.

Sammy, let's make a home where we're happy and comfortable. It'll be based on mutual respect and a lot of love. I know you have it in you as much as I do. Miracles happen. Let's give ours a chance.

Love,
John

Eyes zooming across the computer monitor, Sammy paused, his heart racing, and then went back to the beginning to reread the message. He had to make it make sense.

Sammy sat back in his chair and stared at the screen. Was it true? Was it possible? He desperately wanted to believe him.

For several long minutes, Sammy stared at the screen, rereading the email to decide how to respond. He wanted to convey his hesitancy in moving forward without sounding too mean. He tentatively typed out explanations about misunderstandings and miscommunication, but all of it seemed insincere. In the end, he replied with a short email thanking him and wishing John luck.

On the first Saturday of November, Sammy decided to take an evening walk in the park. Despite the clear sky that forewarned of frostier temperatures, Sammy was content wrapped in his coat. With the full moon shining overhead, Lake Michigan looked like a piece of fine art.

Absent-mindedly, he struck out on a familiar path, the same one in fact that he had often taken with John. He passed the tree where he and John had first sat all those months ago and smiled sadly. After admiring the bare tree for a moment, on impulse Sammy clambered up its knotted trunk and sat on the large, low-hanging branch where he and John had once cuddled.

Peering up at the moon, he breathed deeply the cool air. His heart felt refreshed.

Movement from below caught his attention. Standing beneath him was John.

John regarded him solemnly and then gave a half-smile. "Can… I join you?"

Sammy considered him before holding his hand out. "Yeah."

John climbed into the tree and situated himself on the branch beside Sammy. With a glance, he leaned into him. The smell of his skin sparked something inside Sammy, a kind of aching longing. It wasn't lust, though he certainly had missed the warmth of John's skin.

It was something deeper, something more profound.

Unconditional love.

AUTHOR'S NOTE

The first draft of this novel, which is primarily a work of fiction, was written in 1993. For many years, it was saved in a folder and moved from one computer to another until the fall of 2022, when I was prompted to revisit the manuscript because of the deteriorating state of Palestine. At the time, Gaza had been under siege for years and Israel was pushing into the West Bank, making it impossible for Palestinians to establish an independent state. A year into my revisions, the Gaza War started, adding urgency to my desire to bring a Palestinian narrative into conversation.

After the horrific attack by Hamas on October 7, 2023, which resulted in the deplorable killing and kidnapping of innocent Israeli civilians, Israel responded with excessive and inhumane force. The state of the West Bank rapidly deteriorated; people living in the Gaza Strip fell victim to constant and indiscriminate bombardment that killed tens of thousands of Gazans and injured countless more. Though it is important to condemn Hamas' attack on Israel's sovereign grounds, it is as equally vital to denounce Israel's consequentially over-the-top response. As of the publication of this book, approximately 33,137 Palestinians have been killed in the six months since Israel's war on Hamas began; another 75,815 have been wounded, according to the Associated Press.[1] Nearly 300,000 Gazans

---

[1] Julia Frankel, "Half a year into the war in Gaza, here's a look at the conflict by the numbers," *AP News*, April 6, 2024, https://apnews.com/article/israel-hamas-gaza-war-statistics-95a6407fac94e9d589be234708cd5005?utm_source=Email&utm_medium=share.

face imminent famine.[2] [3] The future of Palestine and its people remains uncertain.

The Israel-Palestine conflict has been the cause of much tension in the Middle East over the years. Since the *Nakba* ("Palestinian Catastrophe") during the 1948 Palestine war, hundreds of thousands of Palestinians have been expelled from their homes and villages to become refugees not only in the West Bank and the Gaza Strip, but also in Lebanon, Syria, and Jordan. Forced to live in deplorable conditions and denied basic human and civil rights, Palestinians have taken the brunt of cruel and unfair Israeli political and religious policies.

The Israeli occupation of the West Bank and the Gaza Strip after the Six-Day War in June 1967; the expansion of Israeli settlements and the confiscation of Palestinian land in violation of international laws that continues to this day; and the denying of Palestinians their right to self-determination has created an environment wrought with conflict, ever-increasing tension, and cyclical hatred and violence. Militaristic responses have not and will not work. All that war has done is deepen the wounds and prolong needless suffering.

In my opinion, the path to peace will be heralded via equality and understanding. All people are entitled to security, prosperity, equality, liberty, and justice. We need to perceive each other as equal human beings. The greatest guarantee for security is to establish a just and comprehensive peace settlement that provides for a viable Palestinian state. We need to discover a way to share the Holy Land amicably.

This novel is a love story that reflects the complexity of intercultural and interreligious relationships. It is not connected to or inspired by the current state of Gaza. In part, it is a reflection of the cumulative experiences of the Palestinian people over decades of oppression. This book exemplifies the human connection between two diametrically opposed men and examines how they navigate the nuanced differences inherent in their respective identities. It is exactly that intimate connection, that cautious curiosity, and respect that, if

---

[2] Jaclyn Diaz, "Famine in northern Gaza is 'imminent,' warns the world's leading authority on hunger," *NPR*, March 19, 2024, https://www.npr.org/2024/03/19/1239394316/gaza-famine-israel-humanitarian-aid.

[3] World Food Programme, "Famine imminent in northern Gaza, new report warns," WFP.org, March 18, 2024, https://www.wfp.org/news/famine-imminent-northern-gaza-new-report-warns.

applied to the greater whole, would move us forward to create a peaceful end to conflict.

ACKNOWLEDGMENTS

Because books are rarely, if ever, a solitary venture, I would like to acknowledge a few people who supported my work.

To Norman Jeddeloh, thank you for your enduring support and generosity. Your guidance and advice have been and continue to be inspirational.

My sincerest gratitude to Sharon Bopp, who was instrumental in the production of this novel. Without her support and effort, this book would never have seen the light of day.

ABOUT THE AUTHOR

Zaman Madhi was born and raised in Gaza. After emigrating to the United States in 1981, he attended American universities where he eventually earned a Master's degree and a Ph.D.

Zaman drew inspiration for this book from the rich cultural scene in Chicago where he lives. He regularly partakes in the diverse and eclectic music scene that exists in the city and is a fan of live theater.